Clan Iver, Peter C. Campbell

An Account of the Clan-Iver

Clan Iver, Peter C. Campbell

An Account of the Clan-Iver

ISBN/EAN: 9783337392956

Printed in Europe, USA, Canada, Australia, Japan

Cover: Foto ©Andreas Hilbeck / pixelio.de

More available books at **www.hansebooks.com**

ACCOUNT

OF

THE CLAN-IVER.

ABERDEEN:

1873.

1. Since the following Work was printed, the Author has ascertained that the Family of Clenary, and consequently of Pennymore, is not, as has been long generally supposed, extinct in the male line, but has living representatives in grandsons of Duncan, the son of the Very Rev. Neil Campbell, Principal of Glasgow College, and Dean of the Chapel Royal. This welcome discovery necessitates the deletion of lines 22 and 23, page 24, and of the latter part of line 18, page 89 ; and an addition to the first paragraph on page 90. Duncan, who was the 5th, not 4th, son of the Principal, (Neil, one of the Clerks of Ordnance, who was the 4th, having been, by a typographical oversight, omitted in the list), had by his first wife, Rebecca Campbell, among other children, a son, also named Duncan, who m. 1st, Harriet, d. of Robert Mylne, Esq. F.R.S., representative of the Mylnes of Balfargie, who from the time of James III. (see Nisbet, vol. i. 125), were for seven generations Royal Architects of Scotland, and by her had:

1. John Campbell, Captain Madras Army, invalided in consequence of illness caused by over-exertion as Assistant-Surveyor-General of the Presidency in connection with the Trigonometrical Snrvey, whom. Maria H. Davis, and has, with three drs., four sons living : 1. Frederick-Duncan, C.E. in the D.P.W. Bombay. 2. Archibald-William. 3. Colin-Charles, Capt. Madras Army (m. and has issue). 4. John Irvine, C.E.

2. Charles-Dugald Campbell, Captain H.M.I.N., now resident at Guildford Surrey, distinguished by his eminent and useful services, especially during the Mutiny, who m. his cousin, Bower-Caroline, d. of William C. Mylne, Esq., F.R.S., and has (with one d., Harriet-Bower), two sons : 1, William-Dugald, C.E., F.G.S. ; 2, Charles.

Duncan (junior) m. 2ndly, Elizabeth Phillips, and had a son now living :

3. Owen-Edward-Collingwood-Campbell.

There may possibly also be issue male of the Rev. Colin C., 3rd son of the Principal, as his son John married, and had two sons.

Duncan Campbell (senior), the Principal's son, married 2ndly Mary Mumford of Sutton-Place, whose family possessed large estates in Kent, and by her had six sons and four daughters. The eldest son, Mumford Campbell, attained a high rank in the Bengal C.S., but, although twice m , died without issue, as did all his brothers. There is issue female of 1st and 2nd Duncan by both their wives.

Duncan 1st was a W.I. proprietor and eminent shipowner, and in the latter capacity was much connected with the Government of his day. He was the original owner of the memorable ship Bounty, and Admiral Bligh, her commander, was in his service before he obtained a commission as Lieutenant in the Navy. Bligh m. Elizabeth Betham, Duncan's niece.

Although not a matter of Clan-Iver history, it may be mentioned, in connection with the paragraph at the head of page 90, that Alexander Campbell, the father of Colin C., who married Henrietta, the daughter of Duncan (senior), appears to have been a son, not, as supposed, of Sir James C., but of Archibald, son of Alexander C. of Strondour, brother of the last Sir Duncan Campbell of Auchinbreck. In either case, Colin was next in the title to the last Sir James.

II. With reference to § v. 3. page 80, the author finds that the officer said to have perished in the Royal George, was not the last descendant of the M'Gilchrists or Gilchrists of Glassary. Besides a d., Jean, who m. a relative of her own name, Daniel or Donald M'G. and Jean Campbell (Duchernan) had two sons : 1. John ; 2. Patrick, alive in 1801, with two sons and two drs. living.

John, the elder son, b. 21st March, 1728, married 1st, 2nd August, 1754,

Margaret, daughter of Muugo Grahame, Esq., and had issue six daughters, of whom two married and had issue; 2ndly, 7th December, 1770, Margaret, only daughter of Robert Ross, Esq. of Auchnacloich in Ross-shire, by his wife Catharine, third daughter of John Mackenzie, Esq. of Highfield, Ross-shire. By her he had four daughters, of whom one had surviving issue, and two sons, 1, Dugald (Major), born 27th July, 1773; 2, Daniel, who died unmarried.

On the death, without issue, 1 Jan. 1797, of his grand-uncle Dugald, the half-brother of his grandfather Daniel, Major Dugald, the elder son of John, inherited the estate of Ospisdale in Sutherland. He m. 25th February 1800, Catharine, elder daughter of Alexander Rose, Esq., H.E.I.C.S., of the Earlsmill or Wester-Clune Branch of Kilravock, and had (with five daughters, of whom Alexandrina-Rose m. William Lyon, Esq. of London, and has issue three sons and three daughters; and Catharine m. George Ross, Esq of Pitcalnie and Amat—): 1, Dugald, W.S., who died unmarried 1834; 2, Daniel, born 1805, who succeeded his father; 3, John, who died young.

Daniel Gilchrist of Ospisdale m. 20th October, 1841, Jane, eldest daughter of John Reoch, Esq. of Gilmerton and Brigton, Co. Fife, and had two sons: 1, Dugald, now of Ospisdale; 2, John-Reoch; and three daughters: 1, Margaret; 2, Catharine-Ross (who m. 1871, Frederick-William Rose, Esq., son of the late Major Hugh St.-Vincent Rose of Calrossie, Ross-shire, and has issue: 1, Frederick-Hamilton, 2, Muriel-Hope); 3, Jane-Georgiana.

Daniel or Donald, who, in 1719, m. Jean Campbell, and his half-brother Dugald of Ospisdale, were the sons of John, the son of Donald M'Gilchrist and Fingwell Stewart. The family ought perhaps to be regarded rather as a collateral than as an offshoot of the Northbar family. The prefix Mac was dropped early in the last century.

III. The author has further to record, with reference to page 58, line 41, that the promising young officer there mentioned, Lieut. Henry-Campbell Macdiarmid, R.E., was carried off suddenly on 7th April, 1873, by solar apoplexy, at Karachi in India, where he had just arrived as Resident Engineer, leaving his only brother, Duncan-Overton Macdiarmid, London, the representative of the family, and the sole surviving descendant in the male line of John Roy Macdiarmid, who was the head of his race in the early part of last century.

ERRATA.

Page 5, line 9, *after* recorded *insert* by.
— 21, — 20, *for* 1725 *read* 1727.
— 21, — 22 & 23 to be *deleted*.
— 36, — 12 from foot, *after* whom *read* with one exception, (*see* Not. to Reader II.)
— 53, — 6 from foot, *after* that *insert* of.
— 56, — last, *for* deem *read* seem.
— 62, — 10 from foot, *for* appreviation *read* abbreviation.
— 74, — 14 from foot, *for* conuteract *read* counteract.
— 76, — 18, *for* faidh *read* faigh.
— 80, — 23, *for* 1803 *read* 1703.
— 86, — 13 from foot, *for* Anna, daughter *read* a daughter.
— 89, — 18, *delete* believed to be extinct.
— 90, — 5, *for* 4, Duncan, *read* 4, Neil; 5, Duncan,
— 90, — 15, *after* Mary, *for* d. unmarried *read* who married Richard Be-
           tham, and had issue; 3, Margaret, who d. unmarried.
— 97, — 8 from foot, *for* Celeraine *read* Coleraine.
— 102, — 12, *for* 1887 *read* 1817.
— 108, — 18, *after* William *insert* Graham.

ACCOUNT OF THE CLAN-IVER.

It is particularly requested that the following correction be at once made with the pen in all the copies issued :—

Page 101, line 26, near the end of the 2nd paragraph—

For Alexander and Roderick, *write* Alexander and Kenneth.

ACCOUNT

OF

THE CLAN-IVER.

HE Clan-Iver, called sometimes Clan-Iver-Glassary, *(Clann-Imheair-Ghlasairidh* or *Ghlasraith)*, from the district of Glassary or Glasrie in Argyllshire,[1]* of which they were for many centuries the principal inhabitants, have been represented in modern times as a branch of the Siol Dhiarmaid,† or Clan-Campbell, and their descent has been deduced from the heads of that Clan, the Black Knights or Lords of Lochawe. But although the Chiefs and the main body of the Clan-Iver have for several generations borne the name of Campbell, and although their alliance with the great House of Argyll, which has existed for many centuries, was strengthened by frequent intermarriage with branches of that house, there can be no doubt that the MacIvers were originally a distinct race, and that, like other ancient families in Argyllshire which have long been merged in the Clan-Campbell, they were induced partly by affection and partly by policy to acquiesce in the genealogical theory, industriously propagated by the Argyll Seannachies, which traced their pedigree to the Lords of Lochawe, and thus, in accordance with the principles of clanship, invested these potentates with the strongest claim on their support.[2] The adoption of this theory may have been facilitated by some previously existing tradition referring the race of Iver and that of Diarmid, from which the Campbells are maternally descended, to a kindred source. It is certain that at a remote period the two races can be traced as near neighbours in the more inland parts of the country. Yet their respective patronymics seem to show the Mac-Ivers to be of Scandinavian and the Macdiarmids of Celtic origin.

* The figures so inserted refer to the Notes in the Appendix.
† Or Sliochd Dhiarmaid.

With still less of good apparent reason, the remnant of the Clan-Iver in Perthshire have sometimes been spoken of as a portion of the Clan-Donnachie or Robertsons of Strowan,* the MaeIvers or Clan-Glasraich of Lochaber, corruptly called Maeglasraichs or Maelaisrichs, as a branch of the Macdonalds of Keppoch, and the MaeIvers of Ross-shire and Lewis as a sept of the Mackenzies. Such very loose statements had their origin in the fact that these detachments of the Clan-Iver, far removed from their own Chieftains, allied themselves to the powerful tribes in whose neighbourhood they were situated, and often ranged themselves under the heads of those tribes in war. These mistakes are, however, the less excusable as these portions of the Clan-Iver did not, like their Chieftains and the main body of the Clan in Argyllshire, exchange their ancient patronymic, which, as a fixed surname, is one of the oldest in the Highlands, for the names of their allies and temporary leaders; and that the Lochaber branch, at least, retained in its designation, Clan-Glasraich, the evidence of its descent from the Clan-Iver of Argyll. A few Perthshire members of the race have indeed in later times been called Robertson in English, but in Gaelic they are spoken of as MaeIvers.

Of the descent of the Clan-Iver from the House of Lochawe, three accounts are given, not only at variance with each other, but all manifestly fabulous, or irreconcilable with known facts. The publication during the present century of ancient records and documents, has in this case, as in many others, exploded legends and genealogies which, in spite of their absurdity, had long found credit.[3]

One of the earliest notices extant of Argyll in a cotemporary public document—the Ordinance of King John Baliol erecting the three Sheriffdoms of Skye, Lorn or Argyll, and Kintyre, dated at Scone, 10 Feb., 1292—shews the descendants of Iver to have been settled there, as an independent family holding their lands of the Crown, in the thirteenth century, thus assigning to them as high an antiquity in that district as can, on any certain historical ground, be claimed for the name of Campbell. By that Ordinance it is decreed that the second of these Sheriffdoms shall comprehend, besides the districts of Kenalbain (Morvern), Ardnamurchan, and Botheluc, the lands of eleven Barons, all mentioned by name, in the list of whom " Malcolm M'Ivyr" is the fourth.[4]

* Stewart of Garth's Sketches of the Highlanders, I. 24.

This notice, viewed in connection with tradition and with still earlier documentary notices at the beginning of the same century, leads to the conclusion that the ancestors of the race were among the Chieftains from the more eastern parts of the country, who, in A.D. 1221, fought under Alexander II. against Somerled the younger, and were rewarded with Baronies in Argyll formed out of the lands which they had conquered, and over which they had established the power of the Crown. This expedition and its results are thus recorded Wyntoun :

> The Kyng that yhere Argyle wan,
> That rebell was til hym before than :
> For wyth his Ost thare-in wes he,
> And Athe tuk of thare Fewté,
> Wyth thare servys and thare Homage,
> That of hym wald hald tharo Heritage :
> Bot of the Ethchetis of the lave
> To the Lordis of that Land ho gave.

Among the warriors of the King's " Ost" on whom the " Ethchetis" or forfeited estates were bestowed, and whose families are found " Lordis of that land" in 1292, were the ancestors of the Macgregors, Macnachtans, and MacEwens, of the Scrymgeours of Dudhope and Dundee, who were already hereditary standard-bearers of the royal army, and, there can be little doubt, also of the, Campbells or Clan-Diarmid,[5] as well as of the MacIvers. In perfect accordance with the narrative of Wyntoun, the tradition of the country relates that Glassary, before it was occupied by the Clan-Iver, belonged to the progenitors of the Macdonalds, that is, the family and followers of Somerled.

Both tradition and historical evidence shew us that the races of Celtic name which bore a part in the conquest of Argyll under Alexander II. were drawn mainly from the nearest Crown-lands in the more eastern districts of central Scotland, particularly from Breadalbane and from the Abthanedom of Dull, comprehending the north-western region of Perthshire, which had become the property of the Crown upon the death of Ethelred, the brother of King Edgar and last Celtic Abbot of Dunkeld.* As the royal army entered Argyll by land, through Strathtay and Glenorchy, (a previous expedition by sea, with forces raised in the south of Scotland, having been beaten back by a tempest), it is obvious that the Crown-vassals of the districts we have mentioned and of the adjoin-

---

* Skene, Highlanders of Scotland, II. 136-7, 168, 201-3, &c.

ing lowlands must have borne a most important part in it. As regards the Clan-Iver, it is certain that they possessed the greater part of Glenlyon in the Abthanedom down to the fifteenth century, from a period so remote that they were traditionally regarded as the first inhabitants after the Fingalians[*] of that sequestered region, which before their arrival in it was called Gleann-Fàsach, or the Desert Glen. The first documental traces of the family of Iver, which are some years older than the conquest of Argyll, connect it both with that part of the country and with the neighbouring districts of Gowrie and Angus.

In the reign of William the Lion, or early in that of Alexander II., " Dovenaldus filius Macvet" [Macbeth] witnesses a charter of Malcolm Earl of Athol granting the Church of Dull, at the entrance to Glenlyon, to the Canons of St. Andrews ;[†] and shortly thereafter, in A.D. 1219, among the witnesses to a perambulation of certain lands belonging to the Abbey of Aberbrothoc, is one who appears to be the same person, styled " Dovenaldus filius Makbeth Macy-war."[‡][6]

The Macbeth of whom Dovenald or Donald was the son, was probably the same who is designated " Judex" of Gowrie and " Vicecomes de Scona" in the reign of William the Lion.[||]

The residence of the body of a family in the highlands of Perth-shire, as immediate vassals of the Crown, is quite compatible with the tenure of office under the Crown by its members or Chiefs in the neighbouring lowlands, then almost equally Celtic, and with their presence there on important occasions ; and the connection of the persons above mentioned with both these districts serves clearly to identify them with the MacIvers who bore a part in the conquest of Argyll, for it is certain that other families from both localities shared in that enterprise, (as well as in a subsequent expedition of Alexander II. into Argyll), and in the advantages resulting from it. The Macnachtans are traced by themselves to the Crown-lands of Strathtay ; and the Macdiarmids, from whom, according to the un-varying tradition of the country, the Campbells are descended in

* New Statistical Account of Perthshire, 530.

† Reg. Priorat. Sti Andreœ, 245, 246.

‡ Acts of the Parliaments of Scotland, vol. I., 81. Votus Registrum de Aber-brothoc, 163.

|| Chart. Coupre, No. 14. Vet. Reg. de Aberbrothoc, 27. Scone was then the capital of Gowrie, which extended from Fortcviot and Mothven on the west, nearly to Dundee on the east, and to Blairgowrie on the north. See Taxatio Ecclesiastica in Vet. Reg. de Aberbrothoc, 238.

the female line, have inhabited Glenlochay and a portion of Glen-lyon, which they shared with the MacIvers, from time immemorial. But it is still more worthy of notice that the Scrymgeours, who were, at the time in question, already established in Gowrie and Angus, and the MacEwens, whose name occurs in both the documents above quoted along with that of Dovenald the son of Macbeth, appear also in the earliest notices of Argyllshire after the conquest of 1221, in the close vicinity of the Clan-Iver in more than one part of that county.* The inference seems unavoidable that the MacIvers whom we find associated with Scrymgeours and with MacEwens both in Glassary and in Cowal after the subjugation of Argyllshire, are the same who are found elsewhere in the neighbourhood of the same families immediately before that event ; and that, whatever may have been their original seat, they were, before arriving in Argyll, connected with Glenlyon and with Gowrie.

It may further be observed that some old Highland genealogies assign a common origin to the MacEwens and the Macglasraichs (MacIvers), deducing them, however, with less evident reason, from Conn of the Hundred Battles, along with the Macdonalds, Macdougalls, Macneils, Maclachlans, and MacEacherns.

It has been conjectured that the Crown-vassals of Breadalbane and of the Abthanedom of Dull who took part in the conquest of Argyll in A.D. 1221, were descended from those Chieftains of Moray whom Malcolm IV., about A.D. 1160, had removed from that province and placed in the Crown-lands in other districts. Such is believed to have been the history of the Macnachtans,† and it must be admitted that the name Iver, which is Scandinavian not Celtic, seems to point to some of those eastern parts of Scotland in which many Northmen, under Thorstein the Red, Sigurd, and Thorfin, obtained a settlement, and, according to the policy natural in such circumstances, endeavoured to strengthen their position by intermarriage with the families of the native Chiefs.

Of Iver, the progenitor of the race which bears his name, nothing is known, nor can it be determined whether he was the grandfather of Dovenald,‡ or whether the patronymic by which Dovenald is distinguished was derived from a more remote ancestor. The Iver

---

* Origines Parochiales Scotiæ, II., 44, 72, 73.

+ Skene, Highlanders of Scotland, II., 167-8, 201-3.

‡ Sir Robert Douglas's statement—which must have been obtained from another source, as he was probably ignorant of the Register of Aberbrothoc—that Iver lived under Malcolm IV. *i. e.* between 1153 and 1165, would, if of any value, lead us to regard Iver as the grandfather of Dovenald.

Crom, to whom the traditions of Argyllshire refer, and who is
famed as the "Conqueror of Cowal," was probably the son of
Dovenald. He must have been posterior by at least three generations to the ancestor who gave his name to the Clan.

The name Iver, which is very ancient and frequent in Scandinavian history, is sometimes used there interchangeably with Ingvar,
of which we may consequently infer it to be an abbreviation. The
old spelling is almost invariably Ivar. In a few instances Iver has
been found. In Scottish writings, as might be expected from the
conflict of different languages and systems of orthography and pronunciation, it appears, like most other proper names, in a great
variety of forms : Ivar, Iver, Ivir, Ivyr, Iuyr, Iwar, Iwer, Yvar,
Yver, Ywar, Ywer, Evar, Ever, Evir, Evyr, Euar, Ewar, Ewer,
Ewir, Ewyr, Ewr, and, in one instance, Urie, evidently a modification
of the diminutive Iverag or Iwerie. The original form Ivar is rare in
Scotland, although its equivalent *Imhear* is found in some old
Gaelic writings. The form Ivor, introduced by the author of
Waverley in the patronymic assigned to his impersonation of a
Highland Chieftain,[7] is not found in old Scottish documents, and
seems to have been peculiar to Wales, into which country, as well
as into Scotland and Ireland, the name was introduced from Scandinavian sources. In the patronymic, all the forms above mentioned
occur after the prefix Mac or Mak, also M'Kiver, Mac Keiver,
M'Kewer, Mac Kyvyr. The branch of the Clan in Cowal pass from
the form M'Iwer, or M'Ewer into M'Cuir and M'Ure, which is the
spelling adopted by John M'Ure, a descendant of the family of Ballochyle, in his quaint but not very accurate work, entitled "A View
of the City of Glasgow," published in 1736, and reprinted in 1830.
He styles himself in Latin "MacIverus alias Campbellus."[*] In
some instances, by the dropping of the prefix, M'Ure has become
Ure, and some families of that name in Dumbartonshire and the
neighbouring counties may be descended from the Cowal Branch of
the Clan-Iver. In the Annals of Ulster and other Irish records,
where the name and patronymic occur very frequently in the notices
of the Scandinavian Princes called Kings of the Gals, from the
ninth to the twelfth centuries, the forms are generally Ivar, M'Ivar,
O'Ivar, passing into O'Hiomhair, O'Hivar, O'Hefare, O'Hair, and
probably into other forms, sometimes ridiculously anglicised Ivers,

---

[*] A Gulielmus Makwre appears among the Masters of Arts laureated in the
University of Edinburgh, July 27, 1611, and an Æneas (Angus) M'Ewer, 12 April,
1687.

Edwards, and Howard! These Irish families have, it is believed, no connection whatever with the Scottish Clan-Iver or its ancestor, being the offspring no doubt of some other Scandinavian adventurer who bore the name. The form M'Keever, in America, is of Irish origin.

When, in later times, it became a fashion to *translate*, as it was absurdly termed, Celtic proper names into English, Iver was sometimes represented as equivalent to Edward and even more strangely to the Greek Evander, with which it has no more connection than other names of Highland origin with their modern substitutes.[8]

IVER CROM, the "Conqueror of Cowal," who is presumed to have been the son of Dovenald, had, according to the universal tradition of the West Highlands, a brother, Tamhais Corr, the progenitor of the sept MacTavish, the Chieftain of which had his seat until a recent period at Dunardary, on the confines of Glassary and Knapdale, and of which there was a branch at Leanach near Strachur. The graves of the brothers are pointed out side by side in the churchyard of Kilmartin, which was in ancient times a favourite burying-place of the chief families that had borne part in the conquest of Argyll.[9]

It may be noted that the name Thomas, from which is formed the Gaelic Tamhais or Tavish, a name at that time rare in Scotland, and probably unknown in the West Highlands, where even now it is scarcely to be found among the natives, adds strength to the evidence which connects the MacIvers with the east of Scotland, where the extraordinary reverence paid at the beginning of the thirteenth century to St. Thomas of Canterbury, the patron of the recent royal foundation of Aberbrothoc, gave early currency to the name. This is a point of some importance when viewed in connection with the presence of Dovenald, the father, as is supposed, of Iver and Thomas, at the perambulation above mentioned of the lands of Aberbrothoc.

Among the lands which, on the expulsion of Somerled and his followers from Argyll, fell to the share of Iver, and formed the barony of his descendant Malcolm M'Iver in 1292, was included the tract lying between Craignish and Kilmelfort, mentioned in charters as the "Dominium de MacIver" or "MacIver's Lairdschip," of which a portion always remained in the possession of his descendants, and from which their territorial designations of Lergachonzie and Asknish were derived. The allotment was an

honourable one, and in accordance with the heroic character assigned to Iver by tradition, being at a point at which the Northmen
and friends of Somerled, whose power was still unbroken in the
Hebrides, could easily approach the coast unperceived under cover
of the adjacent islands, and from which an entrance could rapidly
be made into the very heart of Argyll. Its importance in these
times is marked by the remains of a fortress of considerable extent,
said to have been erected by the Northmen, commanding the bay of
Asknish. The family of Iver also possessed, probably from the same
period, various lands in the parish of Inveraray and in Cowal, the
conquest of which for the king is ascribed to their ancestor, and the
names Baliver, or Iver's Town, at the head of West Loch Tarbet,
and Creagan-Iver, or Iver's Rock, near Strachur, have been thought
to indicate a connection with those parts of the country. To these
was added the important acquisition of the Vale of Glassary, forming
the western portion of the district of that name, in which the main
body of the Clan in Argyllshire always resided, and from which
they derived their well-known designation. Glassary contained
later than the middle of last century no fewer than nine landed
proprietors of the race of Iver, all bearing the name of Campbell, whose forefathers, for the most part, had been in possession of
their estates for many centuries. The MacIver lands in Cowal,
like most of those in Glassary, were very early given off, perhaps
even granted at the time of the conquest, to cadets of the chief
family, as were some of those near Inveraray at a later period.

Soon after the conquest of Argyll, three fortresses were erected
upon Lochawe for the purpose of maintaining the power of the
Crown—Fraochellan at the northern end of the lake, Innisconnell
near the middle, and Finncharn, not far from the southern extremity, where the lake borders the district of Glassary. These
are the three castles on Lochawe mentioned by Fordoun as existing
in his time, that is about A.D. 1385;[*] Kilchurn, although more
conspicuous than any of them, not having been erected till 1440.
Of these fortresses, the first was, by a royal charter still extant, of
date 1267, committed to the keeping of the Macnachtans; the
second was the residence of the Campbells, the Black Knights or
Lords of Lochawe; and that of Finncharn, built, as it would appear
from tradition, on the site of an older fortalice of the family of
Somerled, was held by the Clan-Iver. The Castle of Finncharn,

* Scotichronicon, II. c. 10.

of which the outer walls, remarkable for strength and thickness, are still erect, stands on a small rocky point projecting into the lake, and is said to have been surrounded by its waters before these were lowered by the deepening of their outlet, the River Awe. About half a mile distant is the ruined church of Killineuair or Kilnure, a structure of more elaborate workmanship than was common in that country, within and around which many generations of MacIvers who formerly worshipped there have mouldered into dust. This church, which appears to have been erected after the castle of Finncharn, is said to have been built with stones from Killevin on Loch Fyne, and to have been a parish church and the principal place of worship in Glassary. That distinction, supposed to have previously belonged to Killevin, was transferred, probably at the Reformation, to the more central church of Kilmichael, around which a small town, now entirely decayed, had grown up, and which was the place of sepulture of the MacIvers of Kirnan and other cadets of the race in its neighbourhood. Worship was, however, still celebrated occasionally at Killineuair. The name Killineuair or Kilnure means. Church of the Yew-trees, and is of cognate origin with that of Craigneuair or Craignure in the vicinity.

From their possession of Finncharn and from the tradition of the country, it would appear as if that portion at least of Glassary in which Finncharn lies, and which was for so many centuries possessed by their Clan, must have been originally held of the Crown in free barony by the MacIver Chieftains or some branch of the family, as well as the western estate, or Dominium, of Lergachonzie. The superiority, however, of the greater portion of the district, and the title of Lord of Glassary, are found in 1315 in possession of their allies, the Scrymgeours. That family had already, in 1221, obtained lands in the neighbourhood, which were held by their ancestor, Ralph de Dundee, in 1292, and by his son, John de Glassereth, styled Lord of that Ilk, in 1315. The estate of the Scrymgeours, after having been diminished by the giving off by this John of a marriage portion to his sister, the wife of Dugall Campbell, son of Sir Colin of Lochawe [grandson of Calain-Mòr],[*] was again greatly increased by the acquisition of the Glassary lands of the MacEwens, forfeited in 1371.[†]

In the genealogy of the Clans contained in the MS. of 1450, discovered by Skene in the Advocates' Library and printed in the

---

* Argyll Charters.   † Robertson's Index, p. 59, 10.

Collectanea de Rebus Albanicis, which is regarded by very competent judges as a trustworthy authority in such matters, it is stated that Donald Mac-Reginald, the grandson of the elder Somerled and the progenitor of the Lords of the Isles, had, besides his son by his first marriage, Angus Mòr, another son named John, whose mother was Laliva,[10] the daughter of MacIver. This Donald flourished soon after the period at which we date the settlement of the Clan-Iver in Argyllshire. His eldest son, Angus Mòr, was at the head of the House of the Isles from 1255 to 1292.

IN 1296, about four years after the Ordinance of King John Baliol in which Malcolm M'Ivyr is mentioned, we find King Edward I. ordering "the barons and lieges of Ergile, Nicholas [Neil] Campbell, Baillie of Leghor and Ardescothyn [Lochawe and Ariskcodnish], William de la Haye, Warden of the Earldom of Ross, and the men of that Earldom, to assist Alexander, Earl of Menetcth, then Lord of Knapdale, in Argyllshire, as Warden of the Castles of Ross and Nort Argail," under which last designation was comprehended the whole western portion of the mainland of the present Counties of Inverness and Ross.*

The MacIvers, from the nearness of Glassary to the Earl of Menteith's lands of Knapdale, may be supposed to have borne their full share of the duty thus assigned to them, and in their expeditions to the North most probably originated the permanent settlement, which may be dated from this time, of branches of the family in Lochaber, Glenelg, and Ross-shire, where—especially in Ross-shire—they increased rapidly in numbers and maintained the heroic character of their ancestors, always cherishing faithfully the remembrance of their Argyllshire origin. Of the MacIvers of Lochaber, who in later times were allied to Macdonald of Keppoch, an interesting trait is recorded. When in 1745 they were induced to follow Keppoch to the field, they insisted on forming a separate body and on being commanded by officers of their own name; and when the disposition was made for battle at Culloden, they refused to be placed in a position where they would have had to engage with the militia of Argyll, but demanded to be led on against some other portion of the royal army. Of their subsequent as of their pre-

* Rotuli Scotiæ, vol. I., 32, quoted in Orig. Par. Scot., II., 486.

vious history little is now known. They probably sustained great loss at Culloden. Some of them can be traced in the ranks of the 42nd or Royal Highlanders about thirty years afterwards, and some are believed to have emigrated to America.

Within a century after their settlement in the North, the Mac-Ivers of Ross-shire had attained considerable power and signalized themselves in one of the most desperate conflicts recorded in the annals of the Highlands, the battle of Beallach-na-bròige.* This event, by the very natural mistake of a single figure, has been placed by Sir Robert Gordon in 1275, exactly a century too early, and by others much too late. The true date, A.D. 1375, which alone appears consistent with known facts, is given by Anderson in his history of the family of Fraser, in compiling which he had the advantage of the Fraser, Mackenzie, and Foulis MSS. in the Advocates' Library.† This contest probably originated, like many others, in the opposition of the Highlanders to the rule of a stranger. Sir Walter Leslie, having married Eufame, the only child of William, Earl of Ross, became, on the death of his father-in-law in 1372, possessor of all the power of the Earldom, to the exclusion, contrary to the only principle of succession recognised by the Highlanders, of the male line, which still continued in the family of Ross of Rarichies and Balnagowan, the descendants of the deceased Earl's brother, and the undoubted Chiefs of the Clan-Ross. The result was an insurrection against the new potentate by some of the inhabitants of the Earldom, particularly the MacIvers, Macaulays, and Macleays. The insurgents had formed the design of surprising Lord Ross, but their purpose having become known, Ross seized upon the leader of the enemy, Donald Garve MacIver, and imprisoned him in the Castle of Dingwall. The Highlanders retaliated by seizing Ross's son, Alexander, and carrying him off captive. Lord Ross applied for assistance to the Laird of Lovat, who, it is said, raised 200 of his followers, and with a force consisting of them, the Dingwalls, and the Monroes, pursued the confederate Clans, who were found encamped at Beallach-na-bròige, between Ferrandonald and Loch Broom. A bloody battle ensued, described by Gordon as "a cruel feight, weill followed on either syd." The Clan-Iver, Macaulays, called Clan Talvaich, and Clan-Leay were, Gordon adds, "almost utterlie extinguished and slain." Lord Ross's son was retaken, but "the Monroes and Dingwalls had a sorrowful

---

* Or Beallach-nam-brògan.

† Antiquities of the Shires of Aberdeen and Banff (Spalding Club), II., 386, 387.

victorie, with great loss of their men. Dingwall of Kildun, [Chief of the name] wes ther slain, with seaven score of the surname of Dingwall. Divers of the Monroes were killed, amongst the rest, eleven of the house of Foulls that wer to succeed one after another," and the succession to the Chieftainship of that Clan opened to a child who was then in his cradle.*

Notwithstanding their loss in this engagement, which is no doubt exaggerated, the MacIvers held their position in Ross-shire and recruited their numbers in a few generations. A family of the name is found in the seventeenth century possessed of estates at Leckmelm near Lochbroom, at Midgany in the Abbacy of Fearn or Barony of Geanies, and at Culkenzie in that of Delny ; also of lands named Altnagalloch or Amatnagulloch in Strathoikel.† Another family is said to have been long in hereditary possession (although no charters have been seen) of Arnisdale in Glenelg, and of Letterfearn in Glenshiel, which afterwards settled at Kinlochewe in Gairloch, on the estate of the Mackenzies of Coull. There was in the early part of last century a family of good position known as MacIver of Glenelg. A daughter of Sir Kenneth Mackenzie of Coull, the first Baronet, was married to MacIver of Tournack on Lochewe, and another daughter to Tournack's brother.‡ Other alliances are recorded of MacIvers with important cadets of the House of Kintail or Seaforth, whose standard the MacIvers of Ross appear to have stedfastly followed, in its conflicts with the Macdonalds, Macleods, and others. When, in 1610, the Island of Lewis became the property of Lord Kintail, afterwards Earl of Seaforth, the MacIvers assisted him powerfully in establishing his authority by the sword over the lawless inhabitants, and are said to have been very influential in introducing the Protestant religion and civilisation into the island, into which a great number of the Ross-shire branch of the Clan migrated. In Lewis the MacIvers have always maintained a high character and position. One family, the same above designated as of Tournack, and which held property there down to the middle of the last century, has been settled in hereditary tenancy at Gress for two centuries and a half, from the time of the conquest of the island in which the race bore so important a part. The late Lewis M'Iver, Esq., the eighth representative of this family at Gress, father of

* Gordon's Sutherland, x.
† See Origines Parochiales, II., 470 ; III., 420. Inquisitiones Speciales, II., 83.
‡ Genealogy of the Mackenzies, by the Laird of Applecross, 1661. Douglas, Baronage of Scotland, 401.

Evander M'Iver, Esq., Scourie, is well known as having displayed in promoting agriculture, fish curing, and other arts of peace, the same energy and enterprise for which his kindred in ancient times were distinguished in war. The memory of this gentleman's high character, talents, and public spirit, will long be cherished throughout the island. Another family, originally at Ness and Tolsta, divided into two branches, the one settling at or near Stornoway, and holding the highest position in that part of the island, its members having filled various important public offices; the other at Coll, north of Stornoway. Of these two families, Gress and Ness, which, in the absence of the great feudal proprietors, the Earls of Seaforth, so long and honourably maintained in that sequestered region the dignity and influence befitting gentlemen of ancient blood, as well as of other respectable families of the race in Lewis, many members have from time to time returned to the mainland and proceeded to other parts of the world, where they have occupied positions of great credit and usefulness in professional and commercial life, as clergymen and as officers in the army.

It may be observed that the expedition to North Argyll and Ross-shire in 1296, and the settlement of the MacIvers, and probably of other Argyllshire families, in these countries, may account for the fraternity which appears to have subsisted between some of the maritime tribes of Argyll and the inhabitants of the west coast of Ross-shire, of which the long standing friendship between the Clan-Dugall Campbells of Craignish and the Macraes is a well-known instance. It is probable that the settlement of the colony of Mactavishes in Inverness-shire, where they have long been hereditary occupants of Lord Lovat's lands in Stratherrick on the southern side of Loch Ness, is to be referred to the same time and cause as the migration to the north of their kinsmen, the MacIvers. The like explanation may be given of the settlement of a branch of the Argyllshire Clan Maclachlan at Coruanan in Lochaber.

A T the time of the conquest of Argyll, in 1221, a portion of the Clan still remained in the ancient fastnesses of Glenlyon. They continued undisturbed in their possessions under a local Chieftain styled MacIver of Glenlyon, and in alliance with the powerful Clan of the Robertsons, until some time after the settlement in their neighbourhood of the Stewarts of Fortingal or Garth, when a dispute arose between them and one of the ancestors

of that family, supposed to be the same who is commonly called *an
Cuilean Curta*, the fierce Wolf's Cub, with evident reference to the
well-known title of his progenitor, Alexander Stewart, Earl of
Buchan, the celebrated Wolf of Badenoch. The tradition of the
Garth family, as recorded by the estimable General Stewart of
Garth in his Sketches of the Highlanders,* not unnaturally lays the
blame of the quarrel on the MacIvers; but the violent and rapa-
cious character of their Stewart antagonist, as shewn by his sobri-
quet and still more by the fact, recorded by his descendant, that he
was confined for life by his own friends on account of his ungovern-
able passions and ferocious disposition,† affords room to doubt the
justice of the charge. According to this tradition, which we relate
nearly in Stewart's words, the Laird of Garth had been nursed by a
woman of the Clan Macdiarmid, which was then, and still is, pretty
numerous in Breadalbane and Glenlyon. This woman had two
sons, one of whom, having been injured by MacIver of Glenlyon,
threatened to apply for redress to Garth as his foster-brother; and
the two brothers immediately set out for that purpose to the Castle
of Garth, twelve or fourteen miles distant. In these days a foster-
brother was regarded as one of the family; and MacIver, aware
that the quarrel of the Macdiarmids would be espoused by his
neighbour, ordered a pursuit. The Macdiarmids, being hard
pressed, threw themselves into a deep pool of the river Lyon, into
which they hoped that their pursuers would not venture to follow
them. The foster-brother of Garth was, however, desperately
wounded with an arrow, and drowned in the pool, which, it is said,
still retains the name of Linne Donuil or Donald's Pool. The
other succeeded in reaching Garth. Resolved to avenge his friend's
death, the Laird of Garth collected his followers and marched up
Glenlyon. MacIver mustered his men and met the invaders about
the middle of the Glen. The Chieftains stepped forward between
the two bands in the hope of settling the affair amicably. Garth
took a plaid of which one side was red and the other dark-coloured
tartan; and on proceeding to the conference, he told his men that
if the result was amicable, the darker side of the plaid should remain
outward as it was; if otherwise, he would give the signal of attack
by turning out the red side. It is said that, while they were still
engaged in conference, MacIver whistled loud, and a number of
armed men started up from the adjoining rocks and bushes where

---

* Stewart's Sketches, II., Appendix, viii.   † Ibid, I., 55.

they had been concealed, while the main body were drawn up in front. " Who are these," said Stewart, " and for what purpose are they there ?" ' They are only a herd of my roes that are frisking about the rocks," replied MacIver. " In that case," said the other, " it is time for me to call my hounds " Then, reversing his plaid, he turned to rejoin his men, who had watched his motions and were advancing. Both parties rushed forward to the combat. The tide of battle turned against the MacIvers, the remnant of whom were pursued eight miles farther up the glen. Here they rallied and renewed the unequal fight against their combined enemies, but were again driven back with great loss. The survivors retreated to another part of the country, and were for some time not permitted to return. The names of various spots in Glenlyon are memorials of this sanguinary contest. The scene of the first encounter is called Laggan-a-chatha, or " the hollow of the battle." Leachd-nan-cuaran, " the flat stone of the sandals," is the name of a rock on which one of the parties, according to the custom of the Highlanders, who often fought barefoot, deposited their shoes of untanned leather before the onset; Ruisgeach, " the stripping," is said to be the spot where they threw off their plaids and unsheathed their swords ; and Camus-nan-carn, the " crook of the cairns," the place where the last stand of the MacIvers was made. The number of cairns is pointed to as a proof that that of the slain on both sides must have been great. The loss of the MacIvers is said to have amounted to 140, that of the Stewarts and Macdiarmids is not recorded.[11]

MacIver of Glenlyon's lands, the acquisition of which was probably the chief motive of the attack, were seized upon by Garth, who succeeded soon after in obtaining from King James III. a confirmation of his possession by a royal charter, still extant, dated 24th January, 1477, which General Stewart admits to be the first heritable title obtained by his family to lands in Glenlyon. They did not, however, retain it very long, for, by an indenture dated 15th October, 1488, Neill Stewart of Fortingal or Garth makes over to Sir Duncan Campbell of Glenorchy " the lands and bailliary of Glenlyon, binding himself never in time to come to intromit therewith."* From the tradition of the country, as stated by . General Stewart, some of the MacIvers would seem to have returned to Glenlyon ; but, from the traces found of them, the greater part of the survivors appear to have settled in the Parishes of Kenmore

* Black Book of Taymouth, Appendix, p. 177.

and Killin, allying themselves to the Campbells of Glenorchy, as their kinsmen in Argyle had done to the elder branch of that powerful race. The principal family in these parts is said to have been styled MacIver of Benmore. The appendix printed with the Black Book of Taymouth* contains a Bond of Man-rent by persons of the name to Colin Campbell of Glenorchy, dated 4 Nov., 1552, and others appear in subsequent years as witnesses and parties in various documents. In a Contract of Defence and Bond of Man-rent between Colin Campbell of Glenorchy and the Clan-Lauren, dated Killin, 22 May, 1573, when the Clan-Lauren choose Glenorchy to be their Chief, John M'Yver, and in his absence, Duncan M'Yver, are among the judges appointed to decide in the event of any breach of covenant.† Besides others of smaller note at Kinchrakin and Innerdoquhart, families of MacIvers appear as tenants of importance at Mourlaganmòr in Glenlochay, at Clochran, Port of Tay, and Kenmore, in the Parish of Kenmore, and at Ardchalzie in that of Killin, from 1562 to 1638.‡ When, in 1624, twenty "poind-faulds" are ordered to be erected within the district of Breadalbane, and the superintendence of each is committed to one or two of the chief men of the district, among whom are M'Nab of M'Nab or Bovain, and some cadets of the family of Glenorchy, Duncan M'Ewar is constituted "Principal" of that at Auchmore, and John Dow M'Ewar of that in "the sex-pund-land of Lickis."‖ These persons were probably of the Benmore family. On a Muster-Roll in 1638 of the "haill able men meet to bear arms" within the Parishes of Killin and Strathphillan, Inchadden (Kenmore), Dull, and Weem, among the followers of the Laird of Glenorchy, amounting to about 100, six MacIvers appear as the small remnant of the Clan-Iver in Perthshire, armed after the manner of their fathers with broadsword and target, bow and arrows.§ Of these, five are from the parish of Kenmore, and one from Killin. The grandsons of this small band rendered effective service to the famous John of Glenorchy in the subjugation of Caithness in 1680. Some of the MacIvers of Glenlyon found a home with the Robertsons at Fearnan, near Kenmore, a barony which then belonged to Robertson of Strowan. Members of the race are still to be found in Breadalbane and elsewhere in Perthshire, but in most cases, having assumed the names of Campbell or of Robertson, they cannot easily be distinguished.

---

* Black Book of Taymouth, Appendix 177.   † Ib., 216.   ‡ Ib., 215, 341, &c.
   ‖ Ib., 366.   § Ib., pp. 398, 399, 400, 401, 402.

WE now return to the main body of the Clan in Argyll-shire. About A.D. 1360 or a little later, Iver MacIver of Lergachonzie, the Chieftain at that time, married Christina, heiress of Dugald, Chief of the Clan-dugall or Old Campbells of Craignish, who had been successively the wife of Macdougall of Dunolly, and Macnachtan of Dundarave, and is said in a MS. Account of the Craignish Family, which is not always a safe guide, to have acquired in this manner a portion of the Craignish lands that lay contiguous to his patrimonial estate.[12] It is certain, however, that the only land in the possession of the Chiefs of the MacIvers, which within the period embraced by existing documents can have belonged to the Craignish family, was the single farm of Ardlarach. The remainder of their estate in that district, although lying partly in the *Parish* of Craignish, and partly comprehended in the *later Barony* of that name, held by the Argyll Family, had always been, since 1221, " the Dominium or Lairdschip of MacIver."

Although their progenitor, Iver Crom, was buried at Kilmartin, the MacIvers of Lergachonzie for a long period in later times made the Parish Church of Kilvaree in Craignish their place of sepulture. The old Church or Chapel of Kilbride, situate on their own estate, had probably ceased to be a place of worship and interment before their arrival in Argyllshire, at the time when the parochial system, on the introduction of the Romish polity, superseded the more ancient organization of the Columbite Church. In the Church at Kilvaree, a plain ruin, but beautifully situated and of elegant proportions, there are four stone chests or altar tombs near the eastern end, ornamented with the arabesque sculpture frequent in the West Highlands. Of these the two on the south were the burying-places of the Craignish family, and the two on the north of the MacIvers of Lergachonzie.

The MacIvers always maintained in Argyll the character of a brave and energetic Clan. From the position of their main body between their allies the Campbells, and the Macneills and Macalisters of Knapdale and Kintyre, they were involved in frequent contests with these two Clans, against whom the men of Glassary formed the border guard of the Campbell territory for many generations. The House of Argyll had acquired the superiority of many lands in Knapdale and Kintyre, and being desirous of placing them in the actual possession of their own friends, naturally encouraged the

Clan-Iver to occupy them. At one period the MacIvers were sufficiently powerful to extend their possessions along the coast of Loch-Fyne as far as Loch-Tarbet, and although their tenure of the more distant parts of that country which they had over-run may have been of short duration, and does not appear to have been secured to them by any charter or form of law, yet the fact they effected a settlement and erected a fort on the west side of Loch-Gilp shews that a portion of their conquest must have remained for a time in their possession. At length, as we are informed, the Macneills and Macalisters, pouring into the country in overwhelming numbers, drove back the MacIvers after two bloody conflicts, the former at Lergnahunsion, near the mouth of West Loch-Tarbet, and the latter on the shore of Loch-Fyne. The Macmillans of Knap are said to have assisted the Macneills against the MacIvers at Lergnahunsion.*

Notwithstanding these reverses, the date of which cannot now be ascertained, the MacIvers still constituted a formidable division of the forces of the House of Argyll, which at all times relied with the greatest confidence on the honour and courage of this warlike race. The Chieftains of the Clan were appointed hereditary Keepers and Captains of the Castle of Inveraray, erected in 1432, and it claims the honour of having formed no unimportant portion of the vanguard of the Scottish army on the fatal field of Flodden, at the head of which Archibald, second Earl of Argyll, with his cousin, Sir Duncan Campbell of Glenorchy, and all the flower of Argyllshire, fell valiantly fighting in front of their King.

Long before the close of the fifteenth century, the Clan-Iver in Argyllshire consisted of three distinct Branches:

I. The Branch, or main stem, of LERGACHONZIE or STRONSHIRAY, the head of which, styled simply and *par excellence* " MacIver" or " The MacIver," was always and everywhere recognized as the Chief of the whole Clan-Iver. Of this Branch—the elder line of which, extinct in 1818, bore latterly the designation of Asknish, and will be fully treated of below—were descended:

1. The *MacIvers*, latterly *Campbells*, of *Ardlarach*. The tradition of this family is that they have possessed the farm of Ardlarach, as tenants and proprietors, for about 500 years. They have always been regarded as an offshoot of Lergachonzie, but circumstances create some difficulty as to the precise nature of the connection. Although very remote, *as cadets*, from the Lergachonzie stem, they became nearly

* Statistical Account of Scotland, XIX., 312.

connected with it *in the female line*, by marriage, early in the last century—see Genealogical Tables at the end of the Appendix.

2. The *MacIvers*, latterly *Campbells*, of *Pennymore*, on Loch-Fyne, in the southern part of the parish of Inveraray. Douglas's references to Pennymore are altogether erroneous. He places its origin too late, and ascribes it to a Duncan, followed by an Archibald—names not found in the Pennymore family—and that, too, at a time when the representatives of the family—already in existence for at least two generations—are shewn by charters to have been Iver and John. Yet he seems to have had a sound tradition to rest upon in regarding it as an immediate cadet of Lergachonzie. *Clenary*, in the neighbourhood, appears to have been a sub-cadet of Pennymore, which had branched off from Lergachonzie before 1500. From that date a succession of six proprietors of Pennymore is on record. The direct line of Pennymore ended with William (MacIver) Campbell, whose sister and heiress, Jean, married, first, her kinsman, and probably heir male of Pennymore, Campbell of Clenary, and (after his death without surviving issue) secondly, the Reverend Patrick Campbell of Torblaren (of the Auchinbreck family), by whom she had Dugald Campbell of Kilmory and other children, some of whose offspring rose to great wealth and distinction. Her first husband was succeeded in the representation by his brother, Major John Campbell, executed for partaking in the enterprise of the Earl of Argyll in 1685. The only known son of this brave and unfortunate member of the Clan was the Very Rev. Neil Campbell, Principal of Glasgow College (1725-61), on the expiry of whose male issue in the second generation, the Pennymore family is believed to have become extinct.

3. The *MacIvers Bayne* (Bàn=Fair-haired), or *Feuars* of *Lergachonzie*, descended from Iver-Bayne, a younger son, some time after the year 1500, of the House of Lergachonzie. The genealogy of this family, of which there appears to have been no male issue beyond the fourth generation, will be given below.

4. The *MacIvers Buey* (Buidhe=Yellow-haired), latterly *Campbells*, of *Quoycrook* and *Ducherman*, Chieftains or Captains of the Clan-Iver in Caithness, who deduce their descent from Kenneth Buey, a younger son, near the middle of the sixteenth century, of Lergachonzie, then designated "of Stronshiray." The history of this family also, which claims, as being the nearest cadet, to represent the Lergachonzie Branch since 1818, will be given below.

II. The GLASSARY Branch or Branches, supposed to be descended from cadets of the Clan who bore part in the conquest of Argyll in 1221, or sprang from the Chief House soon after it. In this division, which, from its numbers, gave a designation to the Clan, and which possessed the portion of Glassary extending from the lower part of Lochawe to the river Add, two chief families can be traced for some centuries:

1. The *MacIvers*, or *Campbells*, of *Kirnan* or *Kernanach*. A tombstone at Kilmichael, apparently of about the date 1500, bears the name of ALEXANDER MAK KYIVYR of KEYIRNANAC[H]. In 1581 John Mackewir of Kirnan was the head of this family, which took the lead in Glassary, its representative apparently acting as local lieutenant of the Chieftains, and which may very probably be descended from a younger son or other near relative of Iver Crom. It possessed its property till 1735. Some members of it may still exist in the United States, where they have held positions of distinction. The representative, Frederick

Campbell, assumed in 1815 the additional name of Stuart.   Kirnan has the high honour of having produced Thomas Campbell, author of the "Pleasures of Hope."[13]

2. The *MacIvers*, or *Campbells*, of *Glasvar*, possibly a very old offshoot of Kirnan, whose genealogy can be traced from about 1478 to 1770, after which the head of the family, if still existing, is unknown.   *Letternamolt* (supposed extinct) branched off from Glasvar about 1550, as *Leckguary* is believed to have done about 1690.

The families of *Lagg*, *Achadaherlich*, *Barmolloch*, and *Stroneskar*, proprietors of the lands of these names, all in Glassary, in the sixteenth, seventeenth, and eighteenth centuries, seem to have been sub-cadets either of Kirnan or Glasvar, which two families were probably at one time proprietors of nearly the whole Mac-Iver portion of Glassary; but the relation of these offshoots to them or to each other has not been ascertained.

III. The COWAL Branch, or *MacIvers*, latterly *Campbells*, of *Ballochyle*, probably settled in that district soon after the conquest of 1221.   The first recorded designations of the family were "of Strathauchic"* and " of Dergachie."   It was also sometimes styled " of Kilbride," from the lands of that name near Inveraray, which it held for some generations in the sixteenth century, under the family of Glenorchy as superiors.   The genealogy can be traced from the latter part of the fifteenth century.   Of this Branch were the *M'Ures* of Glasgow, now extinct, and some, at least, of the *Ures* of Dumbartonshire.†   The representative of this Branch, William Rose Campbell, of Ballochyle, Colonel in H.M. Madras Service, died after a few days illness, at Edinburgh, on 22nd March, 1872, leaving an only son, MacIver Forbes Morison Campbell, born in 1867.

The family of *Limekilns*, whose history and descent have not been ascertained, was probably an offshoot of Ballochyle.

The estates of the Chieftains at this time consisted :

1. Of the following lands in *MacIver's Lairdship :* Lergachonzie mòr,[14] Lerga-chonzie bog, Garraran, Asknish, with the islands of Ellan-nan-gaun and Ellan-Craigach, Barvullin, with the Mill of Barvullin, Kilbride, Grianaig, Laganlochan, and also of the neighbouring farm of Ardlarach, which last is described as lying in the Barony of Craignish.   These lands, with the exception of Ardlarach, were originally held of the Crown with the usual baronial privileges, including *mercheta mulierum*, about which much nonsense has been spoken, and the hereditary dignity of Crowner or Toiseadrach within a certain district of Argyll.[15]

2. Of the estate of *Stronshiray* or *Inveraray*, comprehending the lands of Stron-shiray and others in Gleushiray ; the four merklands of Inveraray, which included a portion of the lawn on which the modern Castle of Inveraray is built, and where a large stone still standing erect is said to have been the boundary between the

---

* Strath-Eachaig.

+ The following is a clear instance of the passing of the Cowal form of the patronymic M'Ure into Ure: "Margareta Buchanane, Sponsa Locumtenentis Jacobi Campbell, alias Ure, hœres Joannis Buchanane, Mercatoris Burgensis de Dumbartane, patris."—Inquisit. Gener. 3048, April 3, 1645.

MacIvers and the MacVicars of Stronmagachan, the ten shilling land of Aucharioch, the two other Auchariochs, and various other lands near Inveraray ; the hereditary offices of Captain, Chamberlain, Mayor, and Keeper of the Castle of Inveraray, the lands called the Brewsterland, Maltland, and Peatland ; the fishings of the water of Aray, "as weill heigh as laigh ;" all the other fishings between Auchinbreck and the water of Gerran ; the fishing of Linnequaich, and the salmon fishing of Portanetonaich, near the Kirk of Kilmalew. To these were added, in 1558, the lands of Blarowne, and, in 1562, the lands of Killean and Lealt, in the stewardry of Glenaray, acquired by Duncan MacIver of Stronshiray, before his succession as Chief.*

3. Of some parts of Glassary not yet given away to cadets. But the Craignish MS. errs in saying that Sir Duncan MacIver still held *most* of Glassary in 1581.

When, in the beginning of the sixteenth century, existing documents begin to throw a distinct light on the history of the Clan, we find that the Earls of Argyll, in accordance with their well-known policy, had already obtained a feudal superiority over the lands of the MacIvers, as over the lands of several others of the old Barons of Argyll which had been held immediately of the Crown in 1292. It would further appear about the middle of the same century, that the *calps* of some scattered offshoots of various Clans had begun to be levied or claimed by the Earl of Argyll as landlord. The *calp* was an acknowledgment of clanship, and consisted of the best horse, ox, or cow of a clansman or dependent, which on his decease was claimed by his Chief. It was a principle with the Highlanders to pay this tribute, which was an institution not of the feudal but of the patriarchal system, to him alone who was their Chieftain by blood, whoever might be the feudal superior, or proprietor, of their lands ; and only when a Clan was so much weakened, or "broken," as it was termed, as to render it impossible to establish clearly the right of chieftainship, or when a portion of a Clan had removed to a great distance from its Chieftain, did the members consent to pay their calps to the head of the more powerful Clan to which they were allied, or to their feudal superior. If, as is evident, the object of the House of Argyll was to attach to itself those remote branches of other Clans which had become its feudatories or tenants, and to incorporate them with the Clan-Campbell, it was unwise to attempt this by interposing between them and their hereditary chiefs, and violating a custom to which the Highlanders clung with their characteristic tenacity, and which had with them all the force of a law. The Earl of Argyll therefore, by a formal deed executed in 1564, prudently renounced all claim to any calps of the Clan-Iver in favour of Iver MacIver of Lergachonzie, the acknowledged

* Origines Parochiales Scotiæ, II., 86—90.

Chieftain of the Clan, stipulating only that he should have " the said Iver's calp." By this wise and kindly policy the desired end was effectually attained. By obtaining the single calp of the Chief, he secured the attachment of the whole Clan while respecting their feelings. The practice of levying calps in the Highlands, which on the gradual prevalence of the feudal system gave rise to much contention between chiefs and superiors, was abolished by law in 1617, as it had been in the Celtic district of Galloway upwards of a century before.*[16]

In the year following, 18 June, 1565, this Iver is present at Dunstaffnage at a Council held by the Earl of Argyll " of his barones and gentill his freindis," in which a bond is entered into and signed by the parties present to pursue the Clan-Gregor. The bond is signed by the Campbells of Auchinbreck, Ardkinglas, Barbreck, and Inverliver, by Macdougall of Dunolly, Macnachtan of Dundarave, and MacIver of Lergachonzie. Barbreck, Macdougall, and Macnachtan sign by notary " with their hands on the pen," MacIver and the three others writing their own names. Iver must have been very far advanced in life at this time, as his grandson, Duncan, who succeeded to the chieftainship before 1581, seems to have attained manhood in 1558. It may be here observed that in the genealogy of this family, as of some others given by Sir Robert Douglas, there are, down to the middle of the seventeenth century, so many errors, as shewn by existing documents, as to deprive it of all value.[17]

N OT long after this took place an event of much interest in the history of the Clan ; the appearance in Caithness of a band of MacIvers from Argyll under the leadership of two members of the Lergachonzie family (then designated " of Stronshiray,") Kenneth Buey and his brother Farquhar. The date of this migration may be placed between 1575 and 1585. Kenneth and Farquhar appear in history as " Cheiftanes or Captanes of the Scill-wick-Iver in Catteynes," in 1589 ;[†] but the relations existing in that year between them and the Earl of Caithness, whom they can hardly have known till their arrival in the North, imply that they had already been there for some little time.

Family tradition, corroborated by all the circumstances of the

* Rec. of Privy Council, June 10, July 31, 1617. Acts of Parl., IV., 548.
† Gordon's History of Sutherland.

case, leads us to ascribe this expedition to the influence of Anne or Agnes Keith, Countess of Argyll, eldest daughter of William, the Great Earl Marischal, married first to the Regent Murray, and secondly to Colin, sixth Earl of Argyll, by whose death she again became a widow in 1584. This lady was, like her father, a person of great ability and energy, and during the long sickness of her husband and the minority of her son, directed the counsels and wielded the power of the House of Argyll.* The object of the migration appears to have been the occupation and defence of some estates of the Countess, or her relatives, the Earl Marischal and Lord Oliphant† (who had lands at the time in each of the ten parishes of Caithness) which were then suffering severely from the incursions of the Gunns and other tribes of Sutherland.[18] It was natural that for such an enterprise the Countess should desire the services of the Stronshiray family, so well known to her as the brave and loyal guardians of her husband's castle of Inveraray, and that Kenneth Buey and Farquhar, who as the younger sons of a younger son can have had but little inheritance at home, should become its willing leaders.‡ On arriving in the North, Kenneth and his brother, with their band of MacIvers, soon attracted the notice of the Earl of Caithness, the great local potentate, who, being himself at feud with Sutherland, no doubt found the MacIvers—a race inured to Highland contests— better adapted than his own followers to the predatory warfare that raged with almost incessant fury at this time between Sutherland and Caithness, under their respective Earls. The antagonists against whom the MacIvers seem to have been most frequently pitted were the Gunns, a fierce and warlike race, who, under their chief, patronymically styled MacHamish, formed at this period the border guard of Sutherland on the north-east. Between the two Clans attacks and reprisals continued from the arrival of the MacIvers till 1616. Sir Robert Gordon, the uncle and guardian of the young Earl of Sutherland, who is the only chronicler of these events, ascribes the origin of the quarrels most frequently to the MacIvers, and the praise of victory with equal frequency to their antagonists, who acted under his orders. If it is matter of regret

---

* See "An opinion on the present State, Faction, Religion, and Power of the Nobility of Scotland, 1583."—Bannatyne Miscellany, I. 56.

† The Oliphants were related to the Argyll family as well as to the Countess.

‡ Tradition and circumstantial evidence seem to leave no room for doubt as to the precise place of Kenneth and Farquhar in the family (see below, where the genealogy after 1565 is treated of) ; but direct documentary proof would be welcomed to establish it in legal form, and beyond all possibility of question.

that the only historian who records the actions of the Clan-Iver in
Caithness should be one so little disposed to do them justice, it is at
least satisfactory that we have on record clear proofs and frank
admissions of his unfairness to opponents.[19]

The hostility of the Clan-Gunn procured for the MacIvers the
alliance of the branch of the Mackays known as the Clan-Abarach,
between whom and the Gunns a deadly feud had for some time
existed, and who, although living within the bounds of the modern
county of the name, were at enmity with Sutherland, and allies of
the Earl of Caithness. The Clan-Abarach, with that steadfastness
which seems to have been characteristic of the Mackays, continued
the firm friends of the MacIvers through sunshine and storm.*

One of the events most worthy of note in the contests referred to
happened in the year 1594. In that year the Clan-Gunn invaded
Caithness. Farquhar MacIver, the brother of Kenneth Buey, and
one William Abarach, a great friend of the Earl of Caithness and
of the MacIvers, were guarding the passage of the Water of Thurso
at Polihowar near Harpsdale. While their attention was occupied
with the movements of the enemy in front, another party of the
Gunns forded the river a mile or two further down, and approach-
ing stealthily under cover of a rising ground, made a sudden attack on
them from behind. Farquhar and William made a resolute defence,
but were overpowered by numbers and slain. The spot where
they fell is still pointed out.† Their death was, however, speedily
avenged by their friends, who, marching into Sutherland, attacked
and defeated the Clan-Gunn in Strathie. Seven of the Clan-Gunn
were killed. Their Chieftain, George Mac-Iain-Vic-Rob, and their
greatest champion, Donald Mac-William-Vic-Hendric, who had
been a leader in the attack on Farquhar MacIver, narrowly escaped
with their lives.‡

The lands occupied by the MacIvers in Caithness were in the

---

* Vpon the death of John MacKay, and William Mak-ean-Mack-Rob, followed
the inveterat deidlie fead betweeu the Clan-Gunn and the Slaight-ean-Aberigh.
The long, the many, the horrible euconuters which happened between those tuo
trybes, with the bloudshed and influit spoills committed in every pairt of the diocy
of Catteynes by them and their associats, are of so disordered and troublesome
memorie, that what with their asperous names, together with the confusion of
place, tymes, and persones, it wonld yett be (no donbt) a warr to the reader to over-
look them.—Gordon's Sutherland, 174.

† Gordon calls William, no doubt correctly, a "Sowtherland"; but his popular surname Abarach, and his intimacy with the MacIvers, clearly imply a close connection
by blood or residence with the Clan-Abarach Mackays, the only friends, at the time,
of Caithness, in what is now the County of Sutherland.

‡ Gordon's Sutherland, 199, 207.

Parishes of Halkirk and Reay, not far from Strathic the residence of the Gunns, and extended into the southern extremity of the Parish of Thurso. They appear to have held nearly all the lands within these limits of which the Earl Marischal and Lord Oliphant were superiors.* They can be traced in possession of Quoycrook, with its dependencies, Croytankerrich, Croytvorar, and Polvorar, with the Isle of the same, of part of Braal, of Scots-Calder, Nornis-Calder, and other neighbouring places; and as they also possessed Rumsdale with its extensive shealing, at the southern extremity of Halkirk, it is probable that they held the whole tract in that Parish and in Reay lying between the Waters of Thurso on the East, and of Torran and Forss on the West, excepting the portion between Olgany and Aehrynic bounded by the bend of the Water of Thurso,† and the Episcopal lands of Dorary, which last, however, became afterwards, as will be seen, their principal residence for a time. What portion of these lands, in addition to Quoycrook, from which Kenneth Bucy's family took their designation in Caithness, and which, with other lands near Halkirk, was recovered by his descendant, Patrick Buey Campbell, after 1657, Kenneth held by heritable title, has not been ascertained. It may be presumed, however, to have included the lands of Calder, as tradition says that he and William Buey, his son, at one time resided there. Some of the property was probably possessed in wadset, by far the most common heritable tenure in Caithness at that time. But Quoycrook would appear to have been from the first held by charter, and the new charter obtained by Patrick Buey, in 1674, makes mention of the feu-duty or quitrent previously paid. The title Buey became hereditary in Kenneth's family, having been borne by his successors for several generations, even when not personally applicable.[20]

Kenneth Buey had two sons, William and John.

William MacIver, afterwards Campbell, called William Buey, and sometimes, from his father, MacKenneth or Kennethson, Chieftain of the Clan-Iver in Caithness, was probably the most heroic, as he certainly was the most unfortunate of his race. In 1616, his father being still alive, we find him and his brother John engaged in warfare with Sutherland, against which he maintained the cause of Caithness with the same activity and courage as his father. But

---

* Orig. Par., II., 745, 750, 759, 760.

† In the portion excepted, Wester-Dale, &c., belonged to the Sutherland family, and Dirlet to the Mackays of Farr, in whose Barony of that name it was included. Orig. Par., II., 710-15, 760. Hist. of the House of Mackay, 112, 135.

some years later, about 1623, having quarrelled with Lord Berriedale, son of the Earl of Caithness, who was then administering the
affairs of the Earldom, he was forcibly expelled from his lands, of
which the Earl had now acquired the feudal superiority. Finding
a home for his young family at Achness in Strathnaver, about
twenty miles beyond the Caithness border, amongst the Clan-
Abarach Mackays, the tried friends of his race—whose alliance
with Caithness had been, like his own, recently changed into enmity*—
he returned to Argyllshire, and invoked the aid of the Marquis of
Argyll, then Lord Lorne, who, in consequence of the banishment of
his father, was at the head of the family. Lord Lorne at once recognized the claims on him of a member of the family of Lergachonzie. He espoused the cause of William, (who, as his relations in
Argyll had begun to do, now assumed the name of Campbell), and
commenced negociations with Lord Berriedale on his behalf, writing
also to Lord Gordon and the Earl of Sutherland in the hope of interesting them in his favour. These endeavours, however, proved
unavailing, " William being," as Gordon says, " unreasonable," and
" Berriedale inflexible." Burning with indignation at the ungrateful
conduct of the Caithness family, William Buey resolved to become
the avenger of his own wrongs. He raised in Argyll a body of his
clansmen and of a sept of the Clan-Maclachlan (with which Clan he
is supposed to have been connected by his grandmother), called
MacKinvin,† and, aided by his son-in-law, Gilcolm or Malcolm
Lamont,[21] made four or five incursions into Caithness in as many
successive years, laying waste the lands of the Earldom and carrying off an immense booty. The Earl and people of Sutherland, well
pleased to see the formidable ally of their enemy, the Earl of Caithness, now become his antagonist, favoured William while advancing
and retreating. The history of the Highlands, abounding as it
does in stories of predatory warfare, probably records no parallel to
the boldness, skill, and success with which these repeated forays,
planned and terminating in Argyll, were carried on in the most remote part of Scotland. Lord Berriedale, by influence at Court,
easily got William proclaimed a rebel, and then, as feudal superior,
acquired a legal right to his property in Caithness. At length,
after many victories and escapes, William was caught in an ambus-
cade and put to death, with his eldest son (who, although very young,
had accompanied him in his latest expeditions), and many of his

---

* Gordon's Sutherland. Mackay's History of the House and Clan of Mackay.
† Erroneously transcribed Muckinnon by some writers.

followers, by Lord Berriedale, who, as Gordon says, " so persecuted that race," that they were " almost extinguished." Here, as in the case of the MacIvers at Beallach-na-bròige, Gordon uses the language of hyperbole. Yet it is true that they were reduced for a time to a very small number within the bounds of Caithness.

William's descendants, and some descendants of his nearer relatives, generally bore, as a signature and in formal documents, the name of Campbell which he had adopted, although still for two or three generations frequently called MacIver. particularly in the Highland parts of the country. One family, after bearing for some generations the names Campbell and Iverach alternatively, settled down into the latter form.[22] The descendants of the other members of the race and of the Clansmen who had accompanied Kenneth Buey from Argyll, generally continued, it is understood, to bear that of MacIver, although, after the acquisition, some fifty years later, of the mastery in Caithness by Sir John Campbell of Glenorchy, several of these also are said to have assumed the name of Campbell.

When driven from their homes, some of the MacIvers had, no doubt, like their Chief, found shelter for their families among their friends of the Clan-Abarach. A few, supposed to have been the offspring of John, the brother of William Buey, obtained a footing in Thurso, through the protection probably of female relatives, and appear in the middle of the seventeenth century, under the name of Campbell, at the head of the commerce of that town, then far more important, relatively to the general commerce of Scotland, than it has been for the last 150 years. But the principal rallying point and refuge of the remnant was in lands, not far from their former homes, of which the Earl of Sutherland, now their friend—not Lord Berriedale, their deadly enemy—was the feudal lord. Among these there was a peculiar tract of some eight or ten square miles, named Dorary or the Thicket-Pasture, between the uplands of Halkirk and Reay, yet belonging to neither parish, but which had formed the separate Chapelry of Gavinskirk. This small district, consisting of the Hill of Dorary and the lands skirting its base, had been a shealing of the Bishops of Caithness, and had been sold in 1557, along with the lands and Castle of Scrabster on the coast, by Robert, the Bishop at that time, to the Earl of Sutherland. Dorary had long before been stripped of the woods from which it derived its name, but it had remained untilled and in a state of pasture, although presenting in its lower grounds much soil for cultivation. Here the surviving MacIvers soon found a retreat. Turning their swords into ploughshares, they had, in thirty years after their Chieftain's death, converted a large portion of these neglected slopes into corn-fields, and there, under the names of MacIver, Iverach, and Campbell, lived in peace and comfort, rapidly recruiting their numbers, and maintaining a close intercourse with their burgher kinsmen in Thurso, until better times arose.*

Besides the son who had shared, so young, his father's fate, William Buey seems to have had at least two others; Donald, called by the Highlanders Mac-William-MacIver, and John. He probably had more; but if so, their names have perished. Donald and John appear to have remained, during the greater part if not the whole of their lives, at Achness among their Clan-Abarach friends. The only thing known of them is that they are charged with having taken part in some forays against Sinclair of Dunbeath, in the interest of Lord Reay, in 1666. "Donald Mac-William-MacIver in Achness, and John Mac-William-MacIver there," are included with Mackay of Bighouse, and some of the Clan-Abarach, Sutherlands, and others, in criminal letters issued in consequence of these forays by the Privy Council. Of the children of John nothing definite has been ascertained. But they are believed to have settled at Dorary as they grew up, and to them some members of the race there, and afterwards at Braalbyne, Brubster, and Shurary, may with great probability be traced. Donald, the eldest surviving son of William Buey, had three sons who attained manhood, Patrick of Quoycrook, called Patrick Buey, Farquhar of Rumsdale, and Alexander of Comelfiet.†

Of the early years of Patrick Buey Campbell, who, next after his grandfather, makes a figure as the head of the Caithness branch of the Clan, little is known. Tradition says that on the occasion of the marriage of George, sixth Earl of Caithness, grandson of the enemy of William Buey, to Lady Mary Campbell, daughter of the Marquis of Argyll, which took place at Rosneath, 22 September, 1657, the Earl—anxious, it is supposed, before going to Argyllshire, to conciliate the relatives and friends of William Buey there, and probably at the suggestion of the Marquis of Argyll, who was strongly attached to the MacIvers—sought the attendance of

* It is worthy of observation that in Scrabster, which also was part of the Episcopal property conveyed in 1557 to the Earl of Sutherland, although twelve miles distant from Dorary, Campbells, no doubt of MacIver descent, are found soon after this.
† or Comliofoot.

Patrick, treating him with marked kindness and respect, and putting him in command of a band of young Highlanders, who were to escort his bride and himself as a guard of honour to their distant home. The favourable disposition of the Earl towards Patrick and his family was, it may be believed, fostered by the Countess, and Patrick was soon put in possession of Quoycrook, and other lands adjacent. Owing, however, partly perhaps to the fact that his father was still alive, although unwilling to return to Caithness, but more probably to the great pecuniary embarrassments in which the Earl was, soon after his marriage, found to be involved, no conveyance to him in legal form of any part of the old family estate was executed, or was perhaps possible, until the 27th November, 1674. At that date a new charter, emanating, " with the advice and consent of George, Earl of Caithness," from Sir John Campbell of Glenorchy, to whom his relative the Earl had, in his difficulties, made over in 1670 all his estates and responsibilities for an annuity of 12,000 merks, secured the lands above mentioned to Patrick and his heirs. This property was indeed of small extent as compared with the previous possessions of the family, but along with it there is conveyed to Patrick, by another charter of the same date, a valuable tenement of land and houses at Thurso, which is not supposed to have belonged to them, but which it was more easy for Glenorchy to bestow than it would have been to recover for Patrick more of the family estate from the parties then in possession.

For these conveyances, which were viewed on both sides as an act of, at best, tardy and imperfect justice, no money consideration, as it appears from the deeds themselves, was asked or received. For Quoycrook and the other lands, Patrick is only required to pay a nominal feu-duty of one shilling and sixpence (three halfpence sterling), in addition to a superiority which is stated to have been previously payable to the Earldom out of them, and to have been assigned to the Countess of Caithness as an item in her jointure. Glenorchy had, however, a more important *reddendo* in view. The charter stipulates that " the said Patrick shall be obleist to give his personall presence, *with all others whom he cane command*, at all occasiones when called to go alongst with me against all persones whatsomever (his ma^{tie} being exceptit and forbudit), and that upon their owne propper chairges and expenses."* In the view of Patrick's position as head of the Caithness MacIvers, and of impending feuds, Glen-

* The witnesses are Colin Campbell of Monzie and Colin Campbell of Carwhin, near relatives of Glenorchy, and James Kinnaird of Durwick.

orchy no doubt regarded this as the " valuable consideration ;" while the charter conveying the Thurso property—not for payment—but solely for " good services done and to be done," is evidence of a desire on the part of Glenorchy, who now lived much at Thurso Castle, to facilitate the residence near him of Patrick, whose local knowledge and influence rendered him a valuable counsellor and help.

The accession of Glenorchy to power in Caithness was the beginning of brighter days, not only to Patrick Buey, but to his kinsmen generally. While naturally disposed to befriend an injured race so long and closely connected with his forefathers, and now virtually a portion of the Campbell Clan, Glenorchy could not fail to see the great advantage that must arise from his finding, in a land of unfriendly strangers, a brave and energetic tribe, thoroughly prepared to welcome and support him. He lost no time in doing what he could to redress their wrongs and attach them to himself. The brothers of Patrick Buey, Farquhar and Alexander, were put in possession, the former of Rumsdale in the Highland part of Halkirk, and the other of Comelfict, (which lands, at least Rumsdale, are believed to have formerly belonged to the family), while the cadets of the race, Campbells, Iverachs, and MacIvers, are found spreading, beyond the limits of Dorary, into important holdings in the neighbourhood.*

These acts of justice and favour did not go unrewarded. Glenorchy found the Caithness MacIvers his most valuable and steadfast allies. Patrick, who added great sagacity to the warlike qualities of his race, proved through life the attached and energetic supporter of his powerful friend, and assisted him effectually with head and hand in his contests with the Sinclairs, ending in the memorable battle of 1680. Of the force assembled by Glenorchy on this occasion many were MacIvers from Argyll and Breadalbane, who had not forgotten the injuries done by the Sinclairs to William Buey and their kinsmen. The MacIvers of Caithness, who had collected at the summons of Patrick Buey, were joined by their clansmen from the south. They lodged together in the barns of Quoycrook for some nights before proceeding to give battle to the Sinclairs at Altimarlach ;† and a family tradition used to relate the number of bolls of meal

---

* The Campbells appear in Braalbyne, Brubster, and Shurary ; the Iverachs (or Campbells) in Brachour, Liurary, and Braalbyne ; the MacIvers in Stainland, Skinnand, Waas, &c.

† *Alt-na-mcarlaich*, but worn down to Altimarlach.

from MacIver Buey's girnal that were consumed by them in brose, and baked into bannocks for them by the goodwives of Halkirk. The number is now forgotten. It may have been exaggerated; but it was such as to indicate that either the number or the appetite of the brave Clansmen was considerable. At the battle of Altimarlach or Wick, fought 13 July, 1680, the last Clan-fight (for such it really was) in which they bore a part, and one of the last in the annals of the Highlands, the MacIvers, although forming no very large proportion of the Campbell force of 700, contributed their full share to its triumphant success. The onset, according to uniform tradition, was sounded by the Piper of the Clan in Caithness, Finlay MacIver, who is memorable as having, under the inspiration of the battle-field, extemporized the tune of *Bodach-na-briogais* [23] The Sinclairs, confiding in their superior numbers, were defeated with great slaughter, no fewer than 80 having fallen in crossing the water of Wick, and the MacIvers sheathed their victorious claymores, to be thenceforth drawn only, as they have often been, in the general cause of their sovereign and their country.

After the victory, Patrick Buey appears to have availed himself of the gratitude of Glenorchy, now Earl of Breadalbane, rather for the benefit of his kinsmen than his own. The tenancies of his brothers were converted by Breadalbane into wadsets No record has been found of Farquhar's wadset of Rumsdale, but Alexander's of Comelfict is dated in March, 1682.* Two of his Thurso relatives, William and John, obtained the hereditary posts of Sheriff Clerk and Commissary of the County. The important office of Chamberlain of Caithness, which there is ground for thinking was destined for Patrick's talented son Donald, had he not devoted himself to the Church, was given to his nephew Donald—afterwards of Aimster—the eldest son of Alexander of Comelfict, and was held by him from before 1690 till 1703—his predecessor in that office being William Campbell, the brother, and his successor Duncan Toshach of Monzievaird, the cousin, of the Earl.† William (Roy), Patrick's nephew

---

* This wadset is discharged 23 Feb., 1693-4, by Donald Campbell of Aimster, Alexander's son, and Agnes Charleson, his widow, in favour of John Sinclair of Ulbster, who had purchased Breadalbane's right of redemption.

† If we are to believe Toshach of Monzievaird, Donald of Aimster did not prove very grateful to his uncle. There may have been some jealousy between Aimster and Monzievaird, his successor as Chamberlain, but the latter accuses him in a letter to Lord Breadalbane, of "vitious intromissiones with his uncle Quoycrooke's goodes," after the death of Quoycrook in 1705, and of unkindness to the widow, under pretence of managing for her, in the absence of "Mr. Donald, Quoycrook's sone," who was settled as a clergyman in Argyllshire.

and son-in-law, the son of Farquhar of Rumsdale, acted as factor
over the Highland portion of the estates under his cousin the
Chamberlain.[24]

Of the members of the Clan who had come from the South on
this occasion, almost all soon returned to their homes in Perth and
Argyll, and those of the race since found in Caithness, are probably
all descended from the first migration.[25]

In the peaceful times which Caithness now at last enjoyed,
Patrick Buey devoted himself assiduously to the improvement of
his small estate; and, it is believed, with success.* For although
he did not recover heritably any greater extent of the lands of his
forefathers in that country, he must be supposed, (besides giving
each of his many daughters a suitable dower according to the custom of the time), to have partly provided the means for the additions
made in Argyllshire to the property of the family by his son soon
after his settlement there.† He appears also to have acted as a
Lieutenant and Agent for the Earl of Breadalbane, in the western
part of Caithness, occasionally visiting Edinburgh on the Earl's
business, and a grateful remembrance of his services was retained
by the Breadalbane family for some generations.[26] He died in 1705,
having married Helen Bayne, of the family of Bayne of Clyth or
Bilbster, Chief of the sept of the Clan-Mackay in Caithness descended from John Bàn or Bayne, a cadet of the ennobled House of
Reay. They had several daughters married in Caithness who had
numerous issue, and an only son, Donald Buey, in a letter to whom,
written in 1703, Patrick says he has already " 63 oyes and 5
cir-oyes," *i. e.* grandchildren and great-grandchildren. Of the
daughters, one was married to Murdoch Campbell in Brubster, probably a near relative, and another, Anna, to her cousin-german
William Roy Campbell, above mentioned. The contract of marriage
is dated 3 February, 1689.[27]

Donald Campbell of Quoycrook and Duchernan, known in Caithness as Donald Buey, in Argyllshire as Donald Mòr, the only son
of Patrick Buey, was born at Quoycrook on Lammas Day, 1665.
He appears from an early period of his life to have been seriously

---

* He seems to have left a reputation as an agriculturist, which probably led the
writer of the Old Statistical Account some 120 years afterwards to think him a
farmer, a notion perhaps strengthened by the subject of the fragment of his poem
quoted in the appendix, Note 27.

+ This property, which lay in Glassary, on the east of the River Add, consisted
of the lands of Duchernan, of the Hill of Duchernan, of the lands of Craigmurrell,
of Uila and Miln of Uila, with fishings on the River Add, and the privilege of ferry
over the Add previous to the erection of the bridge.

and studiously disposed. Deep impressions made on his mind by the death of a young companion, and by the scene of carnage which, when not more than fifteen years of age, he had witnessed at Altimarlach, were never effaced; and although full of heredi- tary vigour and activity, powerful in frame, and said to have been accomplished in the athletic and military exercises of his time and country, he resolved to devote himself to a life of peaceful and pious labour. He entered the University and King's College of Aber- deen in 1682, took the degree of M.A. in 1686, and soon afterwards left his home with a high recommendation in Latin, still extant, signed by the Bishop of Caithness (Andrew Wood) and other persons of influence, intending to visit the English and Foreign Universities.[28] How far he accomplished his purpose is not known, but we find him soon afterwards engaged in the study of Theology at the University of Edinburgh. On completing his course he paid a visit to his friends in Argyllshire. It happened that the Parish of Kilmichael-Glassary had recently become vacant. Mr. Campbell was received with open arms by his Clansmen, the MacIver- Campbells of Glassary, and his connections, the Maclachlans and Lamonts, who formed by far the greater number of the heritors and inhabitants, and was invited, with the cordial concurrence of the whole parish, to become its Pastor. Of the MacIvers, some who had fought at Altimarlach, welcomed, it may be believed, with peculiar interest, in his new character as a learned and eloquent spiritual guide, the young representative of their northern kinsmen, whom they remembered as a fair-haired stripling, eleven years before, under the hospitable roof of Quoycrook, and perhaps, young as he then was, as a companion on the field of battle.[29] He was ordained and admitted Minister of the "United Parishes of Kil- michael in Glassary, Kilnure, and Lochgair," on the 31st Dec., 1691. While devoting himself with singular fidelity and success to his duties as the pastor of one of the most extensive and populous charges in Argyllshire, he soon attracted the public notice of the authorities of the Church, and was selected, when still a very young man, for functions of great difficulty and delicacy. His piety and eloquence, and his services to Religion and Education, are still re- membered with grateful veneration in the West Highlands, where many curious anecdotes of him have been handed down; and he was extensively known throughout the Church as the author of "Sacra- mental Meditations on the Sufferings and Death of Christ," and of

E

other practical works. The " Sacramental Meditations," published in 1698, passed through a great many editions, and was one of the most popular manuals of the last century. On attaining manhood, Mr. Campbell, following the custom of his time, always signed himself Daniel, instead of Donald, and his works bear that name on the title page. No member of the Clan-Iver has done it more honour, or is more deserving to be had in remembrance, than the Pastor of Glassary.[30]

Although Mr. Campbell seldom if ever visited Caithness after he left it in 1687, he was not unmindful of the tie that bound him to the relatives and followers of his family in that county. Amongst many other proofs of this, it is recorded that on the occasion of a grievous famine there, by which even persons in easy circumstances were reduced to great temporary straits, he freighted a sloop in the Clyde, and sent it to Thurso laden with provisions for their relief.* He also presented to the parishioners of Halkirk the first copies they ever received of the Gaelic metrical version of the Psalms, in the completion of which he had borne a part, and was long remembered there with gratitude and veneration.

After the death of his mother, who was life-rented in Quoycrook, Mr. Campbell sold the family property in Caithness, which is now possessed by Sir J. G. Tollemache Sinclair of Ulbster, and the connection of the family with that county came to an end, although certain transactions connected with the sale were not terminated till 1743. He died, deeply lamented by his Clansmen and Parishioners, and by the whole Church, on the 28th March, 1722. He married in 1692 Jean, daughter of the Rev. Patrick Campbell of Torblaren, Minister of Inveraray, a cadet of the then powerful family of Auchinbreck, the head of which, Sir Duncan Campbell, Bart., was the principal proprietor in that part of Argyllshire. By her he had five daughters, all married in the county, but of whom there is no surviving issue, and one son :

The Rev. James Campbell of Duchernan, born 1703, admitted Minister of Kilbrandon and Kilchattan in Argyllshire in 1726, married Janet, daughter of his uncle, Dugald Campbell, Esq. of Kilmory, and sister of Peter Campbell, Esq., of Fishriver, Jamaica,

---

* This calamity was the result of a frost on Sunday, 3rd August, 1694, of such severity that the dogs crossed the Pool of Halkirk on the ice. The crops in the west of Caithness, where the MacIvers lived, were completely destroyed. and meal rose to the then enormous price of £8 Scots, or 13s. 4d. sterling per boll. A check was thus given to the returning prosperity of the MacIvers, from which many families never recovered.

from whom descended the late Lady Scarlett, General the Hon. Sir James Yorke Scarlett, G.C.B., the Hon. Peter Campbell Scarlett, C.B., Lord Abinger, the Baroness Strathedcn, and the first Lady Orde of Kilmory. The Rev. James Campbell died on one of the last days of Dec 1742, leaving three daughters, of whom there are now no living descendants, and two sons :

1. Duncan, his heir, of whom below.
2. The Rev. Peter Campbell, born 1739 ; admitted Minister of Kilmichael-Glassary 26th July, 1764 ; died suddenly 19th Feb., 1779 ; married 8th April, 1765, his cousin-german, Margaret, eldest daughter of George Scott, Esq., Comptroller of Customs at Greenock, by Mary, fourth daughter of Dugald Campbell, Esq., of Kilmory. By her (who was born 24th Oct., O.S., 1743, and died 3rd Feb., 1829,) he had (besides several younger sons and daughters who died unmarried, and a daughter, Margaret, who married the Rev. Francis Stewart, Minister of Craignish) :*

   1. John, Merchant in Virginia ; served heir to his father 26th June, 1792 ; died unmarried in Dec., 1796.

   2. James, Lieut. R.N., who was served heir general to his brother John, 16th Nov., 1796, and who succeeded his uncle in the representation of the family—see below.

   3. George, Minister of Ardchattan and Muckairn, Argyllshire (1796-1817), died at Long-Ashton, near Clifton, 31st Jan., 1817, and is buried there. He married, 1805, Jane, daughter of Duncan Macdiarmid, Esq., Glenure, Chief of the " Fair" Macdiarmids, or Macdiarmids of Glenlochay, and had issue :*

      1. Peter-Colin, D.D., Principal of the University of Aberdeen.
      2. Duncan, M.D. Edin., Toronto, Canada ; Vice-President of the Medical Council and College of Physicians and Surgeons of the Province of Ontario.
      3. George-James, died unmarried, 1841.
      1. Margaret.
      2. Grace-Jane.
      3. Augusta-Murray, died young, 1824.

Duncan Campbell of Duchernan was born 1734. After studying for some years at the University of Glasgow, he embraced a mercantile life, and considerably augmented his patrimony by commercial enterprises in America. He then proceeded to Jamaica, where his maternal relatives possessed great estates and influence, and having enjoyed a further period of prosperity, became unexpectedly the victim of negligence and of the misfortunes of a friend, through which, after a legal process said to present some peculiar features, the family property in Scotland was alienated in 1793. He is said to have been an accomplished man, well versed in the languages and literature of modern Europe. He died unmarried, 2d Sept., 1800, leaving only a small property in Jamaica, in respect of

* See Genealogical Tables at the end of the Appendix.

which the present representative of the family was served heir in 1819.* Duncan Campbell of Duchernan was succeeded as representative of the family by his nephew:

James Campbell, Lieutenant R.N., eldest surviving son of his only brother, the Rev. Peter Campbell. Mr. Campbell served with credit in early life in various actions, under Lords Hotham, Hood, St. Vincent, Nelson, and Duncan. He was a junior officer of the Dido, 28, at the time of her memorable action with and capture of the Minerve, 44, and at the battle of St. Vincent; and soon after his appointment as Lieutenant happening, through the absence of his Captain, to be in command of the Victor, 18, at the landing in the Texel, he received great praise for the manner in which he had sustained and directed the fire of that ship in covering the debarkation of the troops. But, losing his health, he retired from active service, and died unmarried 18th Sept., 1818, when the representation of the family devolved on his nephew, Peter-Colin, eldest son of his next and only married brother, the Rev. George Campbell.[31]

RETURNING to the main line of Chiefs at the middle of the sixteenth century, we find the genealogy involved in considerable obscurity. Iver of Lergachonzie, the Chief in 1565, is succeeded in 1572, certainly before 1581, by Duncan, who is designated "of Stronshiray," and also as "Superior of Lergachonzie," held of him under feu-charter (then renewed) by his cousin, Archibald Bayne, as it had been by Archibald's father, Iver Bayne. It is supposed that Iver of 1565, of whom his successor Sir Duncan is rather presumed than certainly known to have been the grandson, had three sons, of whom—1, Duncan, died young without issue; 2, Charles, of Stronshiray, married a daughter of Kenneth Maclachlan of Kellenochanach, or of Inniseonnel, and was the father of Sir Duncan, Kenneth Buey, and Farquhar; 3, Iver Bayne, after the early decease of Duncan, received from his father a feu-charter of part of the old MacIver Lairdship, including the family residence— Stronshiray, which had become more important from its connection with the hereditary offices at Inveraray, being reserved, along with the superiority of the old estate, to Charles, now the elder son

---

* This property, in the parish of St. Anne's, Jamaica, was sold, but the proceeds were lost through the dishonesty of the attorney, who having become embarrassed, decamped on receiving the money to the United States.

of the family. From the circumstance of their possessing and occu-
pying the old family property and seat, Iver Bayne and his son,
Gilleaspuig or Archibald Bayne, although merely *feuars*, were
designated " of Lergachonzie," and it was this, no doubt, that led
Sir Robert Douglas, and others who have blindly followed him, erroneously to insert them in the line of Chiefs.* In 1581, Archibald
Bayne, who had become involved in debt, resigned the " lands of
Askenis, with the yllis of the same callit Ellan-na-gawn and the Ellan
Craigiche into the hands of his cousin and superior Duncan Makewir
of Stonscrow, and Ewar his sone fiar of the samyn," receiving for
the surrender 1200 merks and a renewal of the feu-charter of
" Lergachonzie mòr, Lergachonzie beg, and Grenog, extending to
ten merkland lyand in Makewir of Lergachonicis Lairdschip."
Archibald Bayne had two sons, Dugald, who succeeded him in the
feu of Lergachonzie, and Iver, who appears to have died without
issue. In 1610, Archibald, son and heir of Dugald, having apparently no legitimate issue, with consent of his superior Charles
MacIver, alienates all those lands of the MacIver estate held by him
in feu to Ronald Campbell (Mac-Dhomhnuil-Mhic-Iain) of Barachbeyan, the representative of the Craignish family and the re-
storer of its fortunes, who was the husband of Mary MacIver, only
daughter of Sir Duncan, and sister or half-sister of Charles.

Sir Duncan MacIver of Stronshiray and Lergachonzie,† next Chief
on record after Iver of 1565, was seized in 1558 in " the lands of Blarowne in Glenshera, of the extent of two merklands and a half." In
1562, the Earl of Argyll grants " to Duncan Campbell or M'Keuir
of Stronschero and Katharine Campbell his wife" (supposed to have
been a daughter of Dunstaffnage), " the lands of Killean and Lealt,
in the stewardry of Glenaray, of the old extent of six marks, six
shillings, and eightpence, which had been resigned in the preceding
year by John Campbell, Captain of Dunstaffniche." In 1581,
" Duncan MacIver of Stronshera, Captain of Inverary," obtains
from Colin Campbell of Barbreck a resignation of the lands of
Barvullin. In the same year, in his own name, and that of Ewir
his son, he enters into a contract with Archibald, the son of Iver
Bayne, and Dugald his son, by which, as above stated, Archibald
restores " Askenis with the yllis of the same," on receiving a renewal of the feu-charter of Lergachonzie mòr and beg and Griannig.

* It is strange that Sir Robert did not suspect a genealogy which shewed six
successive generations in a century.

† Orig. Par., Vol. II., 86—90.

In 1602, with " Ewir his oy sone (grandson), son and apperand air
to umquhill Ewir M'Donochy," he grants a wadset, or charter under
right of redemption for 500 merks, of the lands of Ardlarach to
Ronald Campbell of Barachbeyan, the husband of his daughter Mary.*
Duncan is described as " a man of remarkable courage and intrepid-
ity, who was greatly esteemed, and had much of the confidence of
Archibald, Earl of Argyll."† In 1595, he resigned to Earl Archibald the four merklands of Inveraray, the lands of Aucharioch,
the offices of Chamberlain, Mayor, and Keeper of the Castle of
Inveraray, the fishings in that neighbourhood, &c., the cause of the
resignation being, no doubt, the removal of the Earls from Innis-
Connel on Lochawe, to reside personally at Inveraray, which had become the principal messuage of the Earldom.† Sir Duncan married
as his second wife a daughter of the famous Sorley Buey (Somhair-
leadh Buidhe), and sister of the first Earl of Antrim, and is said to
have been forced, through her extravagance and ambition, to sell his
estate and offices at Inveraray, with the exception of Killean. But
the cause of the sale was more probably that which we have assigned.
At the same time, it appears certain that the resources of the family were much diminished in his day. He had two sons, one by his
first wife, named Iver, who predeceased him, leaving a son, also
Iver, described as heir apparent in 1602, but who died without issue
before 1606; and one, most probably by his second wife, named
Charles, who continued the line of the family. He had also a
daughter, Mary, who married, as above stated, Ronald Campbell of
Barachbeyan, and had issue, Donald—killed treacherously when
young, in single combat, by the famous son of Coll-Kitto—John of
Craignish, Farquhar of Laganlochan, and Archibald.

Charles MacIver or Campbell witnesses the contract above mentioned of Duncan his father and Iver his nephew to Ronald Campbell
of Barachbeyan in 1602. In 1610, as Superior, he contracts to infeft
Ronald in the lands of Lergachonzie and Grianaig (ceded by Archibald MacDugall-Vic-Gillespie-Vic-Iver Bayne), to be holden of
him and his heirs on the same terms as by the preceding vassal,
and binds himself not to molest Ronald or his family in the posses-

* The knightly title does not appear in some charters of Duncan's in the
writer's possession. But this omission, which was not uncommon in the case of
the representatives of old families, is unworthy of notice, in the face of the fact
that he is called Sir Duncan by tradition and in the Craignish MS., the author of
which, his descendant, had conversed with persons alive in his lifetime. Possibly
he was knighted late in life, and after the execution of the latest deed which the
writer has seen.

† Douglas, Baronage of Scotland, 538.   Orig. Par., Vol. II., 88.

sion of the same; by which it would appear that he had at first been dissatisfied with the cession of these lands by Archibald his cousin to Ronald, and their permanent separation from the MacIver estate. In 1612, he sells Barvullin, a five merk and forty penny land, to the same Ronald for 2700 merks. In this deed he is designated and signs himself " of Lergachonzie," as being still superior thereof, although in 1610 he is styled " of Asknish." After this time the designation of the family seems always to have been " of Asknish" or " Ashnish." Charles had two sons :

1. Angus, who is styled and signs as "apperand air" to his father in 1612, but who died without issue.

2. Iver, apparently much younger than his brother, by whom the line was continued.

Iver MacIver or Campbell of Asknish is described as " a man of great bravery and resolution, and much attached to the interest of Archibald, ninth Earl of Argyll, which appears," says Sir Robert Douglas, " by many friendly letters from the Earl to him still preserved." When the Earl of Argyll was employed in quelling some civil commotions in 1679, Iver attended him with 100 men of his own tribe, and when the Earl returned from Holland, and engaged in his unfortunate enterprise of 1685, he again joined his standard, although very far advanced in age, and was forfeited along with him.* After the revolution of 1688, when the forfeiture of the family of Argyll, under which had been included the estates of all the vassals of the Earldom who had followed the ninth Earl, was rescinded, Archibald, tenth Earl and first Duke of Argyll, gave back Iver's estates to his son Duncan and his heirs, bearing the surname and arms of Campbell and of the family of MacIver—" *arma et cognomen de Campbell et familiæ de MacIver gerentibus.*"† The statement of Sir Robert Douglas that " before this period they used the surname MacIver, and carried the arms of that family solely," is incorrect; as the name of Campbell had, although not always, yet occasionally been used by the Chiefs, as by all the other members of the Clan-Iver in Argyll, for at least a century previous. Duncan of Stronshiray is styled in 1562 " Campbell or MacIver," and in 1602 he signs himself " Duncan M'Evir Campbell." Iver is forfeited under the name " Iver M'Iver alias Campbell of Arshneish." As regards the

---

* Of the Clansmen who followed their Chief to the field on this occasion, six were taken prisoners " in arms with Argyll," and condemned, with many others, to banishment to the Plantations in America, viz. :—John M'Iver in Tulloch, Malcolm, Angus, Donald, John (2), and Duncan M'Iver. Reg. Privy Council 24th, 30th, and 31st July, 1685.

† Douglas, Baronage, 538.

armorial bearings, it is probable that the crest of the Argyll family, the boars head *couped or*, formerly confined to the MacIvers of Lergachonzie or Stronshiray alone of all the bearers of the name of Campbell, was assumed when the Chieftains became Captains of the Castle of Inveraray, in place of the old MacIver crest, which is thought to have been the hand and dagger, now borne in the second quarter of the first and fourth grand quarters of the shield. The object of the clause inserted at the renewal of the charter was merely to secure the permanency of what had previously rested on custom. Iver was succeeded by his only son:

Duncan Campbell of Asknish, who is said to have been " very active in civilizing the Argyllshiremen."[*] He married a daughter of Macalister of Loup. " an ancient and honourable branch of the Clan Macdonald," by whom he had four sons:

1. Duncan, who succeeded him, but died without issue.
2. Angus, who carried on the line of the family.
3. Malcolm, who died without issue.
4. Donald, described as "a polite, well accomplished gentleman, and much in favour with Archibald, first Duke of Argyll," who likewise died without issue.

He had also a daughter married to Neil Campbell of Ardlarach.

Angus Campbell of Asknish, second son of Duncan, succeeded his brother Duncan, and married Catharine, daughter of Campbell of Dunstaffnage, by a daughter of Buchanan of Leny in Perthshire. By her he had two sons:

1. Angus, his heir.
2. Alexander, who lived at Kilbride, a farm on his brother's estate, and was well known as Alasdair-Dubh-Chilbride. He died without issue, an eccentric and economical old bachelor.

Angus Campbell of Asknish, the elder son of Angus, married Elizabeth, daughter of John Maclachlan of Craiganterve, by Agnes, daughter of Angus Campbell of Skipness, by Jean, daughter of James Stewart, Sheriff of Bute, progenitor of the Earl of Bute. By her he had a numerous issue, of whom six sons and four daughters survived him:

1. Robert, his heir, of whom below.
2. Duncan, Collector of Excise in Perthshire, afterwards at Glasgow, who died without issue, April 1797.
3. Archibald, a midshipman in the navy, died unmarried.
4. Alexander, died young, unmarried.
5. Angus, bred to the sea, perished, unmarried, on board of the Dodington, East Indiaman, in 1755, about 250 leagues east of the Cape of Good Hope.
6. James, an officer of marines, died unmarried.

* Douglas, Baronage, 538.

1. Agnes, m. 1st, John McNab, Surgeon in Inveraray, of whom no issue grew up; 2dly, Walter Paterson, whose descendants now possess the estate.
2. Susanna, m. the Rev. Hugh Campbell, Minister of Craignish, afterwards of Rothesay, but d. without issue.
3. Catharine, m. John Leitch, Merchant in Glasgow, whose issue is believed to be extinct.
4. Isabella, m. Duncan Campbell of Eskart, in Kintyre, and left issue.

Angus, who is said to have been " a man of great probity and honour, and of a most amiable disposition," died in 1746, and was succeeded by his eldest son :

Robert Campbell of Ashnish, Advocate, Sheriff of the county of Argyll, served heir to his father 21st July, 1752. " He was brought up to the bar under the particular tuition of Archibald, Earl of Islay, afterwards Duke of Argyll, and possessed much of the confidence and friendship of that great man as long as he lived."* On the sale of the Auchinbreck estates in 1768, he purchased the estate of Lochgair on Loch-Fyne, and again, near the close of the century, that of Duchernan, in Glassary, the Argyllshire property of his kinsmen, the MacIver Campbells of Duchernan or Quoycrook. In 1769, he married Catharine Eleanora, third daughter and co-heiress of Mail Yates of Maghull, Esq., by Elizabeth, daughter of Humphrey Trafford of Trafford, Esq., both of the county of Lancashire,† and by her left one son, Humphrey Trafford Campbell, and two daughters, Catharine Eleanora, and Sarah Charlotte, who both married but died without issue.[32]

Sir Humphrey Trafford Campbell of Ashnish, Sheriff of Argyllshire, and Convener of the County, born 1770, was knighted on the occasion of presenting an address from the County after the Peace of 1815. He married 27th July, 1799, Elizabeth, daughter of John Williams, Esq. of Ruthyn, Co. Denbigh (who died 6th May, 1819), and had issue a daughter, who died in infancy. On the death of Sir Trafford Campbell, 9th June, 1818, the estates, including the remaining portion of the Lairdship of MacIver, which had been in the uninterrupted possession of the descendants of Iver Crom in the male line for nearly 600 years (from 1221), went, under a settlement made by Robert Campbell of Ashnish, along with his personal acquisitions, to the female branches, passing eventually in 1853 to a family named Paterson, settled in Ireland, descended from a daughter of Angus Campbell of Asknish, who died in 1746, the inheritor exchanging the name of Paterson for that of MacIver-Campbell. By the

* Douglas, Baronage, 538.
† See Debrett's Baronetage, Art. Vavasour.

F

same event, the whole male issue of Sir Duncan MacIver or Campbell of Stronshiray having become extinct, the representation of the ancient House of Lergachonzie and Stronshiray—as Chiefs of the Clan-Iver—devolved *jure sanguinis* on the nearest Cadet of that House, and is claimed as such by the family of Duchernan, formerly Quoycrook, the descendants of Kenneth Buey and Chiefs of the Caithness division of the Clan. The claim, with the grounds on which it rests, was duly lodged and recorded, awaiting the completion of the proof, in the Court of the Lord Lyon in 1854.[33]

THE great misfortune of the Clan-Iver appears to have been the early removal of its branches to parts of the country very distant from each other, and the impossibility of joint action, with the consequent weakness as a Clan, to which this gave rise. Had it not been for this, a race so proverbially brave and active would probably have filled a more conspicuous position in the history of the Highlands.

It is difficult to form a correct estimate of the existing numbers of the Clan. All the MacIvers who remained in Argyllshire having adopted the name of Campbell in the seventeenth century, the connection of their descendants is not always easily recognizable. It is, however, generally known to the individuals themselves, and Campbells are often found who boast of their descent from the families of the race in the Vale of Glassary.

In Caithness, there may be about 200 bearing the names MacIver, Iverach, and Campbell ; and perhaps a greater number descended from this division exist elsewhere.

The number of the descendants of the race in Perthshire, and who trace their origin to the families that remained in that county, is not very great. Several of them bear the name Robertson.

On the mainland of Ross-shire there are several MacIvers in the parish of Gairloch, particularly in the Poolewe district of that parish. There are also still a few families in Lochbroom, Contin, and other parishes. The late Rev. Farquhar M'Iver, Minister of Glenshiel, a descendant of the M'Ivers of Glenelg, used to say that the members of the Clan in Strathconan, in the parish of Contin, were reputed one of the handsomest races in the Highlands. A few offshoots of this division are found in Inverness-shire and elsewhere.

In Lewis, to which the greater number of the Ross-shire Mac-

Ivers appear to have migrated in the seventeenth century, the name and Clan are more numerous than in any other part of the Highlands. At the census of 1861, there were 1072 person of the name in Lewis, chiefly in the Tolsta and Back districts of the parish of Stornoway.

The whole number of the Clan in Scotland, the Colonies, and the United States, may be reckoned as about 2500, of whom more than one-third have long borne the name of Campbell.

There are in Ulster a few descendants of the Clan, as of other Argyllshire races ; but the Irish MacIvers generally have no connection with it, deriving their name from a different progenitor, although, it is believed, they sometimes assume its armorial bearings.

The old war tune of the MacIvers is that generally known by the first line of the words composed to it in comparatively modern times by the Piper of the Clan—*Thoir dhomh mo phiob a's theid mi dhachaidh.* An aged inhabitant of Kilmichael-Glassary, then considerably above 80, informed the writer in 1855 that even in his day no other tune was allowed to be played by wedding processions while entering the village. Any piper who did not pay this act of homage to the Clan was certain of being mobbed, and of having the wind let out of his bag-pipe in a summary manner, by the younger scions of the race. After acquitting himself of this duty, he might play any tune he pleased. It is said, however, that the pipers of the other races around, by whom the Clan-Iver was both feared and respected, willingly joined in recognizing this local prerogative of honour.[34]

There is a curious Gaelic stanza relative to the Clan, well-known in the Highlands, the words of which are supposed to be uttered by the serpent or adder, the only poisonous reptile found in the country :

> Mhionnaich mise do Chlann-Imheair,
> 'S mhionnaich Clann-Imheair dhomh,
> Nach beannaiusa do Chlann-Imheair,
> 'S nach beannadh Clann-Imheair dhomh.

> I have sworn to Clan-Iver,
> And Clan-Iver has sworn to me,
> That I will not injure Clan-Iver,
> Nor Clan-Iver injure me.

The compact recorded in these lines is understood literally by some simple Highlanders, who regard the true members of the Clan as invulnerable by serpents. A friend of another Clan has told the writer that often, when traversing thickets infested by adders in his school-boy days, these lines would come to his mind, and call forth an earnest wish that he had been a member of the favoured race. After much consideration of the subject, the true explanation of the rhyme appears to be that it commemorates an alliance between the Clan-Iver and some other race symbolized by the serpent; and there is every probability that the alliance referred to is that which is known to have anciently existed between the MacIvers in Perthshire and the Clan-Dhonnachie or Robertsons, one of whose cognizances was the serpent, which still appears as one of the supporters in the arms of their Chief, Robertson of Strowan. In some parts of the country the rhyme is found in the following less intelligible form :

> Latha an Fhèill-Bride,
> Their an nathair as an tom :
> Cha bhi mise ri Nic-Imheair,
> 'S cha mho bhios Nic-Imheair rium.[35]

The *Suaicheantas,* or badge, worn by the Clan-Iver in later times, is the Sweet Gale, called also Wild or Bog Myrtle (Myrica Gale), in Gaelic *Roid,* the badge of the Campbells. But there is some reason for believing that it was anciently the Fir-Club-Moss (Lycopodium Selago), in Gaelic *Garbhag-an-t-sleibhe,* which is sometimes said to be a Campbell badge, as having perhaps been the original badge of the considerable number of Campbells who are of the race of Iver.*

The original tartan of the MacIvers cannot now be ascertained. They have long worn that of the Black-Watch, or 42nd Royal Highlanders, which is believed to be the original Campbell tartan, and sometimes latterly that known as the Argyll-Campbell tartan. But a favourite and very proper wear of the Clan, and of the other Argyllshire races who have not preserved their peculiar patterns, seems now to be that which is said to have been adopted, by common consent, on the first embodiment of the Argyllshire Militia. This, which is conjectured to have been the tartan worn, as above-mentioned, by both the Argyll Militia and the MacIvers of Lochaber in the opposite armies at Culloden, is now that of the 91st Regiment, or Argyllshire Highlanders. These tartans, among which the MacIvers are so fortunate as to have a choice, are all of a very chaste and elegant type.

The armorial bearings of the Clan are, as given by Nisbet, I. 30,

---

* Another plant of this genus, the Alpine or Savine-leaved Club-Moss (Lycopodium Alpinum), is said to be the Suaicheantas of the Clan-Macrae.

Quarterly or and gules, a bend sable. The old Crest is supposed to have been the dexter hand in fess, holding a dagger in pale gules, introduced into the second quarter of the first grand-quarter of the shield of the family of Lergachonzie on their assuming the name and arms of Campbell. The arms, as given above, are—suitably differenced—the proper bearings of those branches of the Clan which retain the original patronymic. The Boar's Head crest, assumed by the Lergachonzie family, is, in various forms and tinctures, the crest of many of the branches of the Clan Campbell ; but it was, as above stated, the peculiar distinction of the MacIvers of Lergachonzie, probably as Keepers of Inveraray Castle, to bear it exactly as borne by the Earls of Argyll—*couped or.*

The full armorial insignia of the Chiefs, since the adoption of the name of Campbell, are recorded as follows in the Lyon Register :

Quarterly: First grand quarter counter-quartered ; first and fourth, gyronny of eight or and sable ; second, argent, a dexter hand couped in fess grasping a dagger in pale, gules ; third, argent, a lymphad, or ancient galley, with sails furled and oars in action, sable : Second grand quarter, quarterly or and gules, a bend sable ; Third grand quarter, as the second ; Fourth, as the first. Supporters : Two leopards guardant proper, collared azure, with chains passing between their fore-legs and reflexed over their backs, or. Crest : A boar's head couped or. Motto over the crest : *Nunquam obliviscar*—a reply to the motto of the Earls of Argyll : *Ne obliviscaris.*

During the prevalence of French fashions in the last century, one of the Lairds of Asknish adopted a French version of the motto : *Je 'n oublie pas ;* and had it so engraved on the armorial seal, transmitted by Lady Campbell of Asknish to the writer, after the death of Sir Trafford Campbell. The change, however, does not seem to have been duly authorised or recorded.

The armorial bearings of the family of Duchernan, formerly Quoycrook, or MacIvers Buey, Chiefs of the Caithness division of the Clan, as in the Lyon Register, are the same as the above, the bend sable of the Second and Third (MacIver) quarters being charged with three cross crosslets fitched argent, with the additional motto below the shield : *Per crucem ad lucem.* As above stated, this family claims right to the pure arms and supporters.

William Iverach, Esq. of Wideford, Orkney, on a recent application in the court of the Lord Lyon for recognition as a cadet of the MacIvers Buey of Quoycrook, obtained a right to bear the following arms :

Quarterly: First and Fourth grand quarters as the second and third, Second and Third as the first and fourth, of Duchernan ; the bend sable being engrailed, and

the whole placed within a bordure argent charged with three cushions gules. Crest:
A boar's head couped argent, langued gules. Motto over the crest: *Nunquam
obliviscar.* In this case the Campbell quartering was allowed, as that name was
shewn to have been for some generations borne alternatively by the family, but the
MacIver bearing was placed in the first quarter, that name, in the form Iverach,
having been permanently adopted.

These are the only armorial bearings registered for any members
of the Lergachonzie, Stronshiray, or Asknish Branch.

GLASSARY Branch : No arms are found in the existing Lyon
Register, nor is it known how the paternal shield of MacIver was
differenced as born by this Branch, or how they incorporated the
Campbell arms on adopting the name. The Kirnan family were
in the practice latterly of using a boar's head crest as borne by the
Lergachonzie Branch.

COWAL Branch : The Ballochyle brooch, a very beautiful and
interesting work of the sixteenth century—described and figured
in the Proceedings of the Society of Antiquaries of Scotland, Vol.
I., P. ii., 170—the only old authority known for the arms of this
Branch—was unfortunately left by the maker in a provokingly un-
finished state as regards the armorial decorations. It exhibits a
quartered shield, first and fourth gyronny of eight or and sable, for
Campbell ; but the second and third quarters, which should have
displayed the MacIver coat, suitably differenced, have been left
blank—the engraver probably not knowing the bearings—and were
never filled up. The shield appears twice, in two opposite com-
partments of the eight forming the ornamental border, the com-
partment on the one side in each case bearing the initials M.C.,
and that on the other a leopard's face, perhaps a crest or cognizance, naturally borrowed from the leopards guardant, the supporters
of the arms of MacIver of Lergachonzie, the Chief of the Clan.
The late Colonel William Rose Campbell of Ballochyle, obtained a
right to bear quarterly, first and fourth, gyronny of eight or and
sable ; second and third quarterly or and gules (the MacIver field),
a leopard's face proper. Crest : a boar's head couped proper.
Motto : *I will not forget.*

There is no registration of arms for any special families of the
MacIvers in Scotland who have retained their patronymic. Those
of Ross and Lewis are supposed to have occasionally, and not in-
appropriately, borne in some way or other, as a difference, the *cabar-
fèidh*, or stag's head cabossed, of their great feudal leaders the House
of Seaforth, probably charged on the bend sable, and they now gene-

rally, following the example of their Chiefs in Argyll, use the boar's head crest and the motto latterly borne by them, instead of the old MacIver crest, the hand and dagger.[36]

It ought to be added, in conclusion, that the spelling MacIvor, or M'Ivor, although sometimes seen since the publication of Waverley, was never adopted by any family of position in the Clan in Scotland; and that the first syllable of the name on which the patronymic is founded, is pronounced like the first syllable of *even*, not of *ivory*.

CHRONOLOGICAL TABLE.

REIGNS.	DATES.	
Malcolm IV.	1153-65	Iver, the progenitor from whom the patronymic was probably derived.
William the Lion.	1165-1214	Macbeth MacIver, "Vicecomes de Scona," "Judex de Gowrie."
William and Alex. II.	—	"Dovenald filius Macbeth Mac-Ywar," witnesses the perambulation of the boundaries between the lands of the Abbey of Aberbrothock and Kinblathmont.
Alex. II.	1219	Dovenald witnesses the grant by the Earl of Athol of the Church of Dull to the Canons of St. Andrews.
Alex. II.	1221	Iver (Crom), First Baron of Lergachonzie, and his brother, Tavish (Corr), ancestor of the MacTavishes, take part in the subjugation of Argyll and settle there. Iver "Conqueror of Cowal."
Alex. II.	—	Laliva, daughter of "MacIver," married to Donald MacReginald, progenitor of the Lords of the Isles.
Alex. II. or Alex. III.	1221-92	The MacIvers of the Vale of Glassary (Kirnan and Glasvar) and of Cowal (Ballochyle) probably branched off before 1292.
John Baliol	1292	Malcolm MacIver of Lergachonzie is fourth in the list of the eleven Barons of Argyll at the erection of the Sheriffdom.
John Baliol	1296	The MacIvers of Lochaber, Glenelg, and Ross migrate thither from Argyll.
Robert II.	1361	Iver MacIver of Lergachonzie marries Christina of Craignish.
Robert II.	1375	Battle of Beallach-na-brôige in Ross-shire.
James II. & James III.	1430-1500	The MacIvers engaged in conflicts with the M'Neills and M'Alisters of Knapdale and Kintyre.
James III.	1474	MacIver of Lergachonzie, about this time or earlier, appointed hereditary Captain of Inverarny Castle.
James III.	1476	Battle of Glenlyon. The MacIvers there dispossessed by Stewart of Garth. The remnant remove to Kenmore and Killin.

REIGNS.	DATES.	
James IV.	1500	The MacIvers of Pennymore branch off from Lergachonzie before this date.
James IV.	1513	Battle of Flodden, 9th September.
Mary	1547	Battle of Pinkie, 10th September.
Mary	1564	Iver MacIver of Lergachonzie obtains from Archibald, 5th Earl of Argyll, a renunciation of all claim to the calps of any of the Clan-Iver, Iver agreeing to give the Earl his own calp. He is supposed to have been father of Charles (the father of Duncan of Stronshiray, Kenneth Buey, and Farquhar), and of Iver Bayne.
James VI.	1575-85	MacIvers proceed to Caithness under Kenneth Buey and his brother Farquhar.
James VI.	——	The MacIvers in Argyllshire begin to assume the name of Campbell.
James VI.	1594	The MacIvers in Caithness attacked by the Gunns near Harpsdale. Farquhar Buey slain.
James VI.	——	The MacIvers defeat the Gunns at Strathie.
James VI.	1595	The Earls of Argyll coming to reside personally at Inveraray Castle, Sir Duncan MacIver or Campbell of Stronehiray resigns the hereditary office of Keeper, &c. His descendants assume the title of Asknish.
James VI.	1610	The MacIvers of Ross migrate to Lewis in aid of Lord Kintail, afterwards Earl of Seaforth, under two principal families—the M'Ivers of Gress (of the family of Leckmelm and Tournack in Ross), or Clann-a-Mhaighstir, and the McIvers of Ness or Tolsta, afterwards of Stornoway, or Clann-a-Bhaillidh. Of these two families, and their cadets, most of the MacIvers of Lewis are descended.
Charles I.	1623-28	Quarrel between William Duey MacIver, son of Kenneth Buey, and Lord Berriedale. William expelled from Caithness. Assumes the name of Campbell. His foraye and death.
Charles II.	1657	Patrick Buey Campbell of Quoycrook recovers possession of part of the property in Caithness.
Charles II.	1679	Iver MacIver Campbell of Asknish joins the Earl of Argyll with 100 of his Clan.
Charles II.	1680	Battle of Altimarlach or Wick in Caithness. The Campbells and MacIvers totally defeat the Sinclairs.
James II.	1685	Iver MacIver Campbell of Asknish joins the Earl of Argyll with his Clan, and is forfeited.
William and Mary	1689	Forfeiture of Iver of Asknish rescinded in favour of his son Duncan.
George III.	1818	The male issue of Sir Duncan of Stronshiray becomes extinct on the death of Sir Humphrey Trafford Campbell.

NOTES.

Note 1. Page 3.
Glassary is derived by some from *glas-srath*, green or grey strath, by others from *glas-àiridh*, green hill-pasture or shealing. The modern Gaelic pronunciation, which reduces the word nearly to a dissyllable, *Glassrie*, and the spelling occasionally found in Latin and English documents, *Glassrith* and *Glassereth*, might seem to be in favour of the former derivation. But it is well known how sounds are worn away in common pronunciation in the course of a few generations, and the spelling of five or six centuries ago is no safe guide in etymology—especially in the present case, where, in the names of the Scrymgeours, who were Lords of Glassary in the 13th and following centuries, and a branch of whom took their surname from it, we find it in such divergent forms as *Glacester* and *Glaster*. On the other hand, the term *àiridh*, although perhaps seldom applied to so extensive a tract as Glassary, is abundant in the names of places in the neighbourhood, and is descriptive of the territory in question, which, though containing little level ground, is no where very high, but affords a tract of good pasture for the larger cattle, and appears to have been celebrated for the rearing of horses. On the whole, the preponderance is decidedly in favour of *Glas-àiridh* as the derivation, and *Glassary* as the spelling.

Note 2. Page 3.
It is interesting to observe the assiduity and sagacity with which the House of Lochawe prosecuted for centuries the policy which placed its wise and patriotic Chiefs eventually in the position of local sovereigns of Argyllshire. While with great foresight laying the foundations of their influence in the eye of the Court and of the Law, by securing, through charters—then little valued by Highlanders generally—the feudal superiority of the lands of the ancient proprietors of the soil, they, at the same time, lose no opportunity of basing it, in the meantime, on the Celtic feeling of the country, by allowing currency to theories of remote descent of these proprietors from their own family, and inducing them to adopt the name of Campbell. It was indeed a somewhat difficult task for the Seannachies to affiliate to the House of Lochawe races well-known to have been as long as or longer than itself, independent inhabitants of the country. The method most commonly resorted to was a discovery that a family which it was desirable to affiliate, had sprung from some clandestine and concealed marriage, or some illegitimate connection of a Chief of

G

Lochawe at a remote period—a scheme to which the old Highland custom of hand-fast marriages gave much plausibility and success, especially as the interest of the families in question, and the advantage of securing the protection and favour of the potentates of Lochawe, induced them the more readily to acquiesce in such theories of their descent. At the same time, the tradition of the country always preserved the distinction between the families really of Campbell origin and these other ancient races, and continued long to designate the members of the latter by their old patronymics. Thus, while no doubt has ever been entertained of the Campbell descent of Barbreck, Inverliver, or Ardkinglas, any more than of Glenorchy, Auchinbreck, Ellangreig, Ormidale, Calder (Cawdor), and Lochnell, of some of whom the progeny was very numerous, the tradition is different in the case of the following Argyllshire families:

1. M'Dhonnachie, or Campbell, of Inverawe, with its offshoots, Ducholly, Kilmartin, Shirvain, Southall, &c. Of this family, which possessed the greater part of the magnificent mountain Ben-Cruachan, and which produced many eminent clergymen of the Church of Scotland, and brave officers of the army, the Chief and many members, down to the middle of the seventeenth century, signed themselves M'Dhonnachie, M'Connachie, and Duncanson. In the pedigree of the Maconochies of Meadowbank given in Burke's Landed Gentry (1847), the Inverawe family is derived from Duncan, a son of Sir Neil Campbell of Lochow, by his second wife, a daughter of Sir John Cameron of Lochiel. This genealogy is not more doubtful than that which represents the progenitor of the Meadowbank family, not merely as a member, but actually as the Head of the old House of Inverawe! The undoubted representative of that ancient race is James A. Campbell, Esq. of New-Inverawe. There may be uncertainty as to the precise origin of the Inverawe family. There is none as to its extreme antiquity and position.

2. M'Innes (M'Angus), or Campbell, of Dunstaffnage, theoretically traced to a natural son of Colin of Lochawe, d. 1390, or, as some say, of Colin, first Earl, d. 1492, but perhaps descended from the old Clan M'Innes of Ardgour or Morven. The constabulary of the Castle of Dunstaffnage was, no doubt, bestowed by Robert I. in 1321-22 on an Arthur, and afterwards on an Archibald Campbell; but neither the Seannachies nor the family itself derive the M'Angus Campbells—now and for some centuries of Dunstaffnage—from these persons. The former allege Colin of 1390, the latter Colin, first Earl, to be the progenitor.

3. M'Neil, or Campbell, of Kenmore or Melfort, deduced from a natural son of Sir Colin of Lochawe, d. 1340. This family, which, in the last generation, furnished several highly distinguished officers to the army and navy, although of very doubtful Campbell origin, seems to have no connection whatever with the Clan-Macneill.

4. M'Iver, or Campbell, of Lergachonzie, Stronshiray, and Asknish, one of the Barons of 1292, and the M'Ivers of Glassary and Cowal.

5. M'Dugall, or Campbell, of Craignish, of which the Chief latterly, after the recovery of the estate by Ronald Mac-Dhonuil-Mhic-Iain of Barchbeyan, was called M'Dhonuil-Vic-Iain. This—one of the most ancient families in Argyllshire, the head of it being one of the eleven Barons of 1292—is well known not to be of Campbell descent.

6. M Dhonnachie-Mbòir, or Campbell, of Duntroon. This family is by some supposed to be really descended from a natural son of Colin of Lochawe, d. 1390, but the tradition of a special brotherly alliance between it and the families of Dunstaffnage and Melfort, in accordance with which, on the death of any one of the three, the two others laid the one the head and the other the feet of the deceased in the grave, seems to argue a very ancient community of interest, if not of descent. Of Duntroon the Campbells of Raschoilly, Oib, Tayness, Kuap, and Rudale, were cadets.

7. The Clan-Chearlaich, or perhaps properly Thearlaich—always reputed to be a branch of the Clan-Dugall of Craignish—whose original seat is uncertain. The Chiefs and a considerable number of this race seem to have accompanied the founders of the Breadalbane family into Perthshire, from Glenorchy, where they had been for some generations. They appear in Perthshire as the Campbells of West-Ardleonaig and Corrycharnaig, and are often mentioned also under the names M‘Uairlich and Charliesoun in the Black-book of Taymouth. In Argyllshire, too, they appear of old under the name of M‘Kerliche. The probable Chiefs of this old race are the Inverneil family, re-established in Argyllshire by Sir Archibald and Sir James Campbell.

If to all these we add the number of Macdiarmids who in ancient times, and of Macgregors, Maclarens, and others, who more lately assumed the name of Campbell, it will be seen that many bearing that name in Argyllshire and Perthshire are descended of other races. In fact, prolific as some branches of the Campbells were, it would have been scarcely possible that all the bearers of the name in those counties should have sprung from them.[*]

A similar aggregation of large numbers from different races took place in many other cases, as in those of the Frasers, Gordons, &c.; but, while in these instances, the persons incorporated seem to have been mainly *nativi* without property, or members of broken septs, the Argyll family succeeded in attaching to itself and engrafting many old, independent, and well organized small Clans. If there is evidence of good policy here, there is also indubitable proof of the hereditary possession by the Black Knights of Lochawe, of the qualities that attract admiration and confidence.

It will be observed that almost all the families enumerated above are found in occupation of prominent and commanding points of Argyllshire—chiefly on the coast—a proof of early possession and power. It must also be borne in mind that, although not of the Campbell race, they almost all had latterly, through marriage with branches of the Argyll family—zealously promoted by the House of Lochawe—a large infusion, in many cases ultimately a preponderance, of Campbell blood.

Note 3. Page 4.

The first is that Buchanan of Auchmar [Brief Enquiry. p. 30.] who makes Iver and his brother Tavish illegitimate sons of Colin of Lochow, styled *Maol* or the Bald. This Colin is said by some to have been killed at Dunstaffnage,

---

[*] There is a third Argyllshire family of which the Head was styled M‘Dhonnachie—Campbell of Glenfeochan. This family may probably have sprung from the House of Lochawe, but the writer has not traced its descent with certainty.

while King Edgar, who died in 1107, was there ; and by Buchanan himself he is married to a niece of Alexander I., or II., and made King's Lieutenant in Argyll—which could not be before 1221—while at the same time he is represented as great-great-great-grandfather of Calain Mòr, who was certainly killed in 1292! This descent, from Calain Maol, seems to have been the favourite theory of the Argyll Seannachies. It places the origin of the Clan-Iver in a period so very remote and obscure as to escape severe criticism. Its gross inconsistencies are, however, self evident.

The second is that given in a genealogical table prefixed to his Life of Archibald Duke of Argyll and Greenwich, by Robert Campbell of Kirnan, who being himself of the race of Iver, and apparently desirous at once to retain the Campbell theory, and to get rid of the notion of illegitimacy, makes Iver and Tavish the sons of Archibald of Lochawe about 1360, " by a daughter of the Thane of Knapdale (Suaine Ruaidh), whom he afterwards repudiated." If anything were necessary to show the worthlessness of a theory no where else mentioned, and the author of which evidently wishes (although he does not venture to say it) to convey to his readers an impression that his own family, Kirnan, were the heads of the Clan-Iver, it is enough to point out that it places the birth of Iver, the progenitor of the race, nearly seventy years later than the period, 1292, at which his descendants are now proved to have been already Barons in Argyll.

The third account is that given by (or rather furnished to) Sir Robert Douglas, and which styles Iver the son of Duncan, Lord of Lochow, who, according to the MS. history of the family [*penes* Macmillan of Dunmore] was son of Sir Archibald, or Gillespic, second son of Malcolm of Lochow, by the heiress of Beauchamp in France [a peculiar form of the Beauchamp theory of the etymology of Campbell], who was a sister's daughter of William the Conqueror!

A fourth genealogy, which deduces the House of Lochawe in an unbroken male line from Constantine the Great, through King Arthur, who is represented as Constantine's great-grandson, makes Iver and Tavish the sons of a Sir Duncan of Lochow, the nineteenth from Constantine, and the brother of Colin Maol!

It is, in the present day, scarcely conceivable how men could commit such absurdities to writing.

Note 4.   Page 4.

Dominus Rex pro pace et stabilitate Regni sui observand. statuit et ordinavit quod de Terris subscriptis fient [vicecomitatus] videlicet. De terra Comit. de Ros in Nort Argail . Terra de Glen . . . Terra Reg. de Skey et Lodoux . Octo davaux de terra . . . . . . Egge et Rume Guiste et Barrich cum minutis insulis . et vocetur Vicecomitatus de Skey.

De terris Kinnelbathyn . Ardenmurich . Bothelue . Terra Alex. de Argadia . Terra Joh. de Glenurwy . Terra Gilberti Mc . . . . . Terra *Malcolmi McIvyr* . Terra Dugalli de Craigins . Terra Joh. McGilc'st . Terra Magri Radulphi de Dunde . Terra Gileskel McLachl . . . . . . Terra Comit. de Meneteth de Knapedal . Terra Aneg. fil. Dovenaldi Insularum . Terra Colini Cambel . Et vocetur Vicecomitatus de [Lorn].

De terris de Kentyr cum omnibus tenentibus terras in eadem . Terra Lochmani McKilcolmi McErewer . Terra Eneg. McErewer . Terra de . . . . . . Insula de Boot . Terra dom. Thom. Cambel . et Terra Dunkani Duf . et vocetur Vic. Kentyr. *Acta Parliam. Scot.* I. 91. *Origin. Paroch.* II. 109.

The eleven Barons mentioned within the sheriffdom of Lorn are—

1. Alex. de Argadia—Chief of the Macdougalls.
2. Joh. de Glenurwy—Chief of the Macgregors.
3. Gilbert Mc[Ewen]—most probably the Chief of the McEwens of Otter, who had also possessions on the opposite side of Lochfyne, held of the Crown, and forfeited before 1371.
4. Malcolm McIvyr—Chief of the MacIvers.
5. Dugall de Craigins—Chief of the Clandugall of Craignish.
6. Joh. McGilchrist—Chief of the Macnachtans. The Chief in the preceding generation is known to have been Gilchrist, to whom, in 1267, the keeping of the Castle of Fraochellan was committed.
7. Radulphus de Dunde—the progenitor of the Scrymgeours of Dundee and Dudhope, who became Lords of Glassary after the conquest in 1221.
8. Gileskel McLach[lan]—Chief of the Maclachlans.
9. The Earl of Menteith.
10. Angus, son of Dovenald (Donald) of the Isles.
11. Colin Campbell, Calain Mòr, whose family was destined to rise very soon to the head of the list of Barons of Argyll.

Note 5. Page 5.

The origin of the race and name of Campbell has been much discussed. The present writer, after considering the subject in every light he could think of, arrived long ago at the conclusion that both are of Norman. at least not of Highland origin. He has found nothing to shake his opinion.

It is agreed on all hands that the first bearer of the name of Campbell in Argyll married Eva. the heiress of Paul MacDhiarmaid, called Paul-an-Sporran, the Chief of the Siol-Dhiarmaid. and transmitted her inheritance to their common progeny, the Black Knights of Lochow. The question is—Who was this Campbell ?

The Argyllshire Seannachies in deference to the Celtic feeling, which recognized no succession except in the male line, are found giving currency to the belief that this first Argyll Campbell—whom they name, no doubt correctly, Gillespic—was a relative of his wife—that he was in fact the *heir male* of the race of which she was the *heiress of line.* But, with their manifest unity of purpose, there is some difference of detail in their accounts.

1. Some represent Gillespic as a Macdiarmid, who had obtained, by certain services in France, an estate. which gave him the name of de Beauchamp. From the latinized form of this—*de Campo bello*—the name Campbell is said to have been derived.

2. Others, varying the legend, make Gillespic the son of a Macdiarmid, an adventurer in France, by the heiress of an estate named Beauchamp, who

they are good enough to inform us, was a sister or near relative of William the Conqueror. The Beauchamp fable appears also in other slightly varied forms.

3. A third party, taking the bull of Norman descent in the male line by the horns, deny any connection with France at all, and maintain that the first bearer of the name Campbell was a pure untravelled Highlander of the same race, whose name, Campbell, was originally a personal epithet—a mere nickname—derived from *Cam*, crooked, and *bèul*, mouth.

To every form of the Beauchamp theory it is a sufficient answer that, while the latinized form, if we judge by analogical cases, would rather have been *de Bello-Campo* than *de Campo-Bello ;* the common appellation of the race must evidently have been founded on what was the name as currently borne by them, and not on its form *as translated into Latin.*

Of the derivation from *Cam* and *bèul*, crooked mouth, it may be said that while it is impossible for any one to prevent the popular application to himself of a name founded on a personal deformity, no one in the position of the early Lords of Lochow is likely to have humbly *accepted* such a name for himself and his family. On indicating this objection to the derivation of the name from *Cam* and *bèul*, the author has been referred to the alleged analogous case of Cruickshanks. The instance is an unfortunate one ; Cruickshanks, as is well known, being derived from no personal deformity, but from *Crux-Sancta*, or rather *Croix-Saincte*. Some good natured supporters of the *Cam* and *bèul* derivation of Campbell, endeavour to make it more palatable to the hearers of that name, by suggesting that it is taken, not from any *deformity* of the mouth, but from the beautifully traced curve of the upper lip by which—as the author has been told is believed in Ireland—the Campbells were distinguished. The sugges-tion is a kindly one, but it cannot procure acceptance for the etymology it is made to support. To that etymology the decisive answer is that the name is not, and never has been, pronounced *Cam-bhèulach*, as it must have been, had the derivation been well founded, but *Caimball* and *Caimballach*.

The name Cameron, and its imaginary derivation *Cam-shròn*, have been quoted in support of the etymology of Campbell under discussion. If Cameron is supposed to have been taken from *Cam-shròn* in the sense of *wry nose*, we may at once pronounce its adoption impossible. But we are told that *Cam* may have been employed in the better sense of *aquiline* or *hook-nosed.* To this we reply that the term employed in that case would have been not *Cam* but *Crom-shrònach.* We are not here discussing the origin of the Camerons. But we believe the theory to be true which derives the first bearer of that name from the south, and represents him as the husband of the heiress of a Highland Chief.

Such marriages—with heiresses—could not possibly have taken place in any part of the Highlands before the feudal law of succession had been established over the patriarchal ; for until then there were no heiresses to marry ; the Celtic law and custom excluding all female succession to land. Now, this change did not take place in Argyllshire until the conquest of 1221, frequently referred to in this volume, and which has not been sufficiently adverted to as the date of a great revolution in that part of Scotland. The marriage, therefore, of Eva Macdiarmid, *as an heiress*, must have taken place subsequently to that event.

It is impossible to discuss every point minutely in a note, nor does it deem neccessary to do so. The true state of the case has long appeared to the author to he as follows. The army with which Alexander II effected in 1221 the conquest of Argyll, was, as has heen stated at pages 6 and 7, collected partly in Perthshire—the MacIvers, Macdiarmids, Macnachtans, and MacEwens, of Glenlyon and Strathtay, hearing part in it—and partly in Angus, from which the warriors of non-celtic race—the Scrymgeours of Dundee, and others, came. Without dwelling much on the fact that there appears about that time, in Angus, a family named " de Camelyn," or arguing strongly for the identity of this family and the Campbells, there is every probability that the first Campbell in Argyllshire—where there is no historical trace of the name until several years later than 1221—was one of those who joined the expedition from Angus, and that his own share of the conquered lands of Argyll was augmented hy his marriage with the daughter of his companion in arms, Paul-an-Sporran, the Chief of the ancient race of the Macdiarmids.

As to the previous history of the Campbells, the author is strongly of opinion that the original of the name is *Camville* (written sometimes Campville and Canville)—a name which appears in the rolls of Battle Abhey, and which was held by least two families of note in England for several generations after the Norman conquest. These families are derived by the French genealogists from the manor of Camville in the Bailliary of Caux, on the road from Rouen to Fécamp. But there are no fewer than five manors of the same name in Normandy mentioned in D'Expilly's Dictionnaire de la France, besides two of the name of Campville. These names would run easily into Camhel—the original form in which the name appears in Scotland—and strong analogical support might be found for the derivation in other instances where the terminal *ville* has hecome *bel* or *ble*. The writer, on mentioning this derivation of the name to the late Lord Chancellor Campbell, had the pleasure of learning that his Lordship had arrived at the same conclusion as to its probability.

A further and, to persons accustomed to such investigations, very strong proof of Norman origin is found in the name Colin, which is confined in the 13th century, when it first appears, very sparingly, in Scotland, to the Campbells, and one or two families of undoubted Norman descent. The name Colin has been identified with Colm or Columba—an etymology of which the only origin seems to he the absurd patronymic Maccallummore—founded on the vulgar low country mispronunciation of Mac-Calainmòr—unfortunately employed hy Sir Walter Scott, and persevered in. after remonstrance, hy Macaulay. Colin is simply the old Norman abbreviation of Nicolas—one of the most common christian names along the continental shores of the Channel and the German Ocean. Of thirty-four persons named Nicolaus in Latin in a Roll of the Ban and Arrière-Ban of a part of Normandy in the 13th century, the author has found no fewer than twenty-six named in French, *Colin*, and three named *Colart*.

It is curious to observe here that not only the frequently recurring and characteristic name *Colin*, but that of *Neil*, which occurs, in one instance, in the line of Lords of Lochawe, are from the same source—*Nicolas*. In that instance, the name is not the Celtic or Norse *Nial*. This is proved by the fact that the bearer of it, Sir Neil Campbell, son of Colin Mòr, is styled Nicolas in Balliol's Ordinance of 1296, and Nicol in the Ragman Roll.

It is impossible to fix the time, between 1066 and 1221, at which the progenitors of the Campbells crossed the Border. The Celtic name Gillespie, borne by the first who settled in Argyll, implies that he was a native of Scotland—and the fact that no fewer than seven persons named Cambel in different parts of the country, appear on the Ragman Roll seventy years after the introduction of the name into Argyll, is scarcely reconcilable with the supposition that they were all descended from from the House of Lochawe *after* that event, although their descendants acknowledged that House as the Head of their name and race.

There is indeed a tradition that the Black Knights of Lochawe were not always regarded, even in Argyllshire, as the Chiefs of the name, but that this position belonged to the Campbells of Strachur, known patronymically as Mac-Arthur, from their progenitor of that name. This notion appears to be founded in a mistake. There was a very ancient Highland sept in Argyllshire named M'Arthur, represented by the M'Arthurs of Innistraynich and Tiravadich, totally distinct from the Campbells, and who are traditionally regarded as deriving their name and descent from King Arthur. A pedigree originating at such a depth in the past, gave rise to the well known distich :—

> Cruic a's uile a's Alpanaich :
> Ach cuin a 'thainig Artaraich?
>
> Hills and Ills and MacAlpins ;
> But when came forth the MacArthurs?

This hyperbolical allusion to the antiquity of the sept McArthur, seems to have been transferred to the *Mac-Arthur Campbells* of Strachur, and the notion has thus been encouraged of their being at least more ancient than all the other Campbells.

The Macdiarmids in Argyllshire, after the death of Paul-an-Sporran, seem to have followed the husband of his daughter as their *Leader*—although not their proper *Chief*—and to have eventually recognized him in the latter capacity—applying to his descendants, as to themselves, the title of Siol or Sliochd-Dhiarmaid. But although this designation has long been regarded as equivalent to Clan-Campbell, it must not be forgotten that a remnant of the ancient race of Diarmid, in the male line, still continued under its old patronymic, in or near its former seats, Glenlyon and Glenlochay in Perthshire —see pages 16 and 17 of this work. Of this there were two branches, known as the Fair and the Dark Macdiarmids. Of the Chiefs of the former—which always held the precedency—the line of succession since the Reformation has been carefully preserved. The Head of the Family at that time was Gilleaspuig, whose succession is indicated by the following pedigree of his representative—Duncan Macdiarmid, Esq., who removed from the old residence of the family, Kenknock in Glenlochay, to Glenure in Argyllshire, and died there about a hundred years ago. That gentleman (whose great grandson, Henry Campbell Macdiarmid, Lieutenant R.E., now represents the family) was styled Donncha-Bàn-Mac-Iain-Ruaidh, Mhic-Dhonncha, Mhic-Fhionnlaith. Mhic-Aonghais, Mhic-Eoghain-Bhàin, Mhic-Ghilleaspuig.

Note 6. Page 6.

Carta Malcolmi Comitis de Athol de ecclia de Dul.

Omnibus Scte Matris ecclie filiis Mulcolmus comes de Athoil Salutem . Sciant

tam presentes quom futuri me dedisse et concessisse et hac mea carta confirmasse Deo et ecclie Scti Andree apli in Scocia et canonicis ibidem deo servientibus et servituris eccliam de Dul cum capellis et terris et cum omnibus ad eam juste pertinentibus in liberam et perpetuam elemosinam post decessum Willelmi clerici mei pro salute anime mee et Hextilde comitisse sponse mee et pro animabus patrum et matrum et omnium antecessorum nrorum . Quare volo et precipio ut predicti canonici predictam ecclesiam et omnia ad eam juste pertinencia ita libere et quiete teneant et possideant sicut aliqua alia elemosina liberius et quiecius tenetur et possidetur in toto regno Scotorum . Si quis autem hanc donacionem meam infringet aut aliqua ex parte minuere attemptaverit meam plenariam maledictionem habeat . Testibus Dunecano Comite de Fif . Hextilda Comitissa sponsa mea . Michaele clerico . Henrico et Dunecano filiis meis . Malcolmo MacEwen . Glinn filio Gilandres . *Dovenaldo filio Mac Vet* . Hugone aurifabro de rokesburch . Magistro Adam de Sancto Andrea. Elia capellano. *Registrum Priorat. Sti. Andreae,* 245, 246.

Perambulacio facta inter Terras quasdam Monasterii de Aberbrothoc et Baroniam de Kinblathmund . A.D. 1219.

Anno ab incarnacione domini M.CC°.XIX°. vicesima tertia die Septembris per hos ambulatores subscriptos . Gilpatrik Mac Ewen . Dunachy filium Gilpatrik . Malcolmum fratrem Thayni de Edevy . Gillecryst filium Ewen Costr' . Gillecryst hominem Comitis de Anegus . Keraldum fratrem Ade judicis . Matheum filium Mathei filii Dusyth' de Conan . iuste et secundum assisam terre perambulate fuerunt recte divise inter Kynblythmund et Adynglas et Ahirhrothoc scilicet Hathuerbelath' usque ad Sythnekerd et sic ad caput Munegungy . Et hii tunc presentes fuerunt . Hugo de Cambrun vicecomes de Forfar . Anegus filius comitis Gilbryd de Anegus . Robertus de Inuerkelethir . W. de Monte alto . Adam de Neveth . *Douenaldus filius Makbeth MacYwar* . Johannes abbas de Brechyn . Morgundus filius ejus . Adame de Bonuill . Robertus de Rossyn . Duncanus de Fernevel . Adam Senescallus de Aberbrothoc . Thomas filius Roberti filii Ade Gar' . Gilys Thayn de Edevy . Nicholaus braciator regis . Rogerus marus Episcopi Brechinensis . Walterus de Baillol . *Hec perambulacio in hunc modum inventa scripta est in rotulis Domini Regis.—Acts of the Parliament of Scotland, Vol. I. p. 81. Vet. Regist. de Aberbrothoc,* 162, 163.

The name Macbeth, or Magbeth, it may be observed here, is peculiar, inasmuch as while from its form it might appear to be a patronymic, it is used as (and probably really is) a Christian or first name. If not, it is a very rare instance in these times of a surname used as such. Chalmers mentions several persons of distinction who bore it in the reigns of Alexander I., David I., and William the Lion, and employs the fact that men of rank gave that name to their sons, as a proof that the real character and position of King Macbeth were very different from those of the Macbeth of the drama. The truth seems to be that Macbeth was the exponent of the Celtic feeling and law in opposition to the feudal, and the ultimate prevalence of the latter sufficiently accounts for the traditional character given him. *Caledonia,* I., 402.

H

Note 7.   Page 8.

No member of the race of Iver can feel otherwise than grátified that the great and much-loved Sir Walter Scott should have selected their patronymic (although under an unusual spelling) as the name of his magnificent impersonation.

At the same time it is singular that he should have given to a Jacobite Chieftain a name which, with the single exception explained in page 12, adhered in all parts of the Highlands to the cause of Protestantism and of the House of Brunswick with a steadfastness rarely shewn by the Highland Clans in any cause whatsoever, and which was exemplified on the same side only by the Campbells, the Mackays, and the Munros, which two latter Clans have inscribed their names in indelible characters on noble pages of the military history of Germany and Protestantism.

Sir Walter, although he caught and embodied with magic power the spirit and customs of the Highlands, seems to have made no very minute enquiry into its local history and the relations of the septs to each other.

In his Rob Roy, c. xxix., Sir Walter puts into the mouth of a Highlander named Allan Iverach, the words : " Our lochs ne'er saw the Cawmil lymphads." The lochs nearest to the Iverachs (MacIvers) were in reality those best acquainted with the lymphads; and no Highlander would have used the vulgar low-country pronunciation " Cawmil."

It may seem scarcely worthy of mention here—but similar and much worse mistakes have been been made by writers of a different stamp from the Author of Waverley. In a novel entitled " Allan Breck," which fell under the present writer's observation many years ago, and which turns on the incident of the dastardly murder in Appin of Colin Campbell of Glenure, by the hand of an assassin named Allan Breck Stewart, the name of Macdiarmid—than which certainly a more ancient and well-sounding, and as certainly a less Jacobite, name could hardly be found—is applied to a race evidently meant as the Stewarts of Appin! This might be passed over as a blunder, and sheltered under the example of the similar mistake of Sir Walter Scott, but the author has been guilty of something not so venial, in grossly misapprehending the position and character of Allan Breck's victim—a gallant soldier, a man of high endowments, cultivated by study and travel, and whose philanthropic efforts for the improvement of the Highlands, made his death to be felt as a lamentation and a dishonour by all the respectable Jacobites of the West Highlands, no less than by his own friends. Glenure, who had served in the Royal Army during the war of 1745, as an officer of Loudon's Highlanders, withdrew from the service to accept the appointment of Factor on the Forfeited Estates in the West Highlands, for the very purpose of serving and protecting his unfortunate neighbours, the Stewarts of Appin, and his cousin-german, Cameron of Lochiel, with their tenants, during the forfeiture. The kindness with which he discharged his trust, and the benefits conferred on the district by his great and judicious improvements—witness the planting of the Lochiel estates—are too well known to need any notice, and one of the most beautiful and touching poems in the Gaelic language is the well-known lament of Duncan Bàn M'Intyre, no anti-Jacobite, over this murdered friend of the Highlanders of whatever clan or party. This is the man whom the author of " Allan Breck"

represents as a vulgar and greedy pettyfogger of twice the age which the assassin's bullet allowed Colin of Glenure to attain.

One unfortunate feature there indeed was in the sequel to this brutal murder —that, by the escape of Allan Breck, the penalty of capital punishment fell only on one—James Stewart—who, although he appears to have deserved his fate. was not the principal criminal, and that he was tried before the Duke of Argyll, the Chief of the Camphells, as the Heritahle Grand Justiciary of Argyllshire.

Note 8. Page 9.

Some of the " translations," as they are called, of Highland names are not the less ludicrous for heing familiar. Thus, to give a few instances :

Angus, a Pictish name, anciently Ungus, becomes Æneas.

Aodh, possibly the Odo, Eudes, Otto, Otho, of Middle Europe, appears not merely in the reasonable forms of Y and Odo, but in those of Hugh, Eugene, Idoneus, and actually of Diogenes!

Eachan becomes Hector. Hippias or Philip would have heen more proper.

Donald hecomes Daniel.

Peter is given as equivalent to Patrick. The name Peter, which was found, though rarely, of old, in the Highlands, and always in the form Malpeder or Gilpeder, has entirely disappeared there ; hut the Patricks, who are numerous, are frequently called in English Peter.

Somerled—Scandinavian—has become Samuel. Thormod is changed to Norman.

In Ireland matters are carried to even a greater degree of absurdity— Murdoch or Murtagh hecomes Mortimer, Diarmid becomes Jeremiah and Darby, while Malachi, Terence, Darcy, Cornelius, and a host of other Scriptural, Latin, and Norman names and surnames, do duty for old Celtic appellations.

Even in Scotland there are some received *equivalents* which are extremely remarkable, as they cannot have originated in any similarity of sound. What can have been the connection between Gillcaspuig (scrvant of the Bishop) and Archihald—hetween Maoldomhnaich (devotee of Dominic) and Lewis ?

Note 9. Page 9.

The descendants of Iver having discontinued (see p. 19) to hury at Kilmartin, the sepulchres of the hrothers were left entirely to the M'Tavishes of Dunardary. At no very remote period, one of that family was interred under the tomhstone not of his progenitor but of Iver, or, as some say, Iver's stone, a larger and finer one than that of Tavish, was placed over him hy the M'Tavishes. Resistance was offered by some MacIvers present, and the stone was somewhat injured in the struggle. But the stronger party on the spot prevailed, and, to secure their triumph, inscribed in modern capitals the name M'Tavish over the hreast of the knightly figure on the tombstone of Iver.

This, as is well known. is not the only stone among the many fine old Highland monuments in the churchyard of Kilmartin, the chief hurying place in the thirteenth and fourteenth centuries of many great families of Argyll, which has been appropriated and defaced by the inscription of names of other families in modern characters.

At the same time, in justice to the McTavishes, it ought to be said that although their ancestor did not attain, like his brother, a baronial position in Argyll at the Conquest, or the same increase of progeny afterwards, they always sustained the character of a brave and honourable race. Their situation, as severed by the Moss of Crinan from their friends, laid them more open even ,than the MacIvers of Glassary to the hostility of the tribes of Knapdale ; and it is much to their credit that the Chiefs maintained themselves in possession of their old seat of Dunardary till near the close of the last century. Like the Clan-Iver, they adhered stedfastly to the other descendants of the Conquerors of 1221, and to the House of Argyll; and Dugald McTavish of Dunardary, as is well known, was brutally hanged from the battlements of the Castle of Carnasary, in Kilmartin, while acting as an officer of the garrison under Sir Duncan Campbell of Auchinbreck, by the Jacobite invaders of Argyll in 1685.*

Although the McTavishes never assumed the name of Campbell, they latterly used as their arms, although probably without any sanction from the Lyon Office, the gyronny of the Campbells (changing the tinctures into *argent* and *azure*), and the boar's head crest. Unfortunately, in accordance with the poor taste of later times, some members of the Clan " translated" their patronymic into the English equivalent Thomson. The consequence has been, that many persons of the latter name, of Low-country origin, and totally unconnected with the Clan Tavish, have usurped the above armorial insignia.

Note 10. Page 12.

This name, of which the derivation is probably *lamh-liamh*—smooth or polished hand—is one of those beautifully descriptive and euphonious Gaelic female names which a wretched modern taste has abolished, or, which is much worse, "translated," like Highland names of men, into others in more common use, but not always bearing much resemblance to them even in sound.

Of the few still in use, the following are the best known :—

Aoibhê, *elegant*, in the form Eva.

Aoibhir, probably the same in root and meaning, best known by the compounds Aoibhiràluin, Evirallin, *beautiful Evir*, and Aoibhir caomha, Evircoma, *gentle or beloved Evir*.

Aoife, supposed from Aoifi, *sweet*. This name, borne by Cuchullin's wife, appears now as Effie ; and Effie being also the well known low-land appreviation of Euphemia or Eufane, these names, of Greek origin, have been sometimes improperly adopted, as well as the familiar form Phemie, by bearers of the Celtic name of Aoife.

Beathag, diminutive from beatha, *life*, appears latinized as Bega, in old Scotch as Bethoc, in modern Scotch or English as Bethia, Beatrice, and Becca, from which it passes on to Rebecca !

---

* See " Depredations on the Clan Campbell." The passages referring to this event are more accessible in the excellent and interesting article on Kilmartin in the New Statistical Account, by the Rev. Donald M'Calman of Drishaig, then incumbent of Kilmartin, now of Ardchattan.

Cairasdionn is always rendered Christiana or Christina, but the identity is doubtful.

Dirbhàil or Derbhàil, and Derforgealla, in Latin Dervala and Devorgilla, are modernized into Dorothea, Dorothy, and Dolly!

Fionnmhala, Fionnlamh, and Fiounghala. The first portion of these names and of some others, is fionn, *white*, compounded with mala, *brow*, lamh, *hand*, and probably guala, *shoulder*. They all appear in Latin and English as Finvola, Finola, and Fenella. The last—Fionnghala—which seems to have been the most common in Scotland, appears as Fingwell, Phinguel, Penuel, and Penelope; but most frequently, during the last and present centuries, as Flora, with which, of course, it has no connection whatever.

Gràine, probably connected with gràdhan, *beloved, darling*, has given way entirely to Grace.

Gormla, *blue eye*, or *blue lady*, still maintains its proper form in the few instances in which it is found.

Mìna, *smooth*, has of late become Minna.

Malvina, *smooth brow*, has been restored to use by the publication of Ossian.

Reullura, *new* or *bright star*. This name, saved from extinction by the poet Campbell, who saw its beauty, is rare. It is probably the name now represented by Laura, when found in the Highlands, and by Lura in Ireland.

Sileas, *peace*, the Irish Sheelah, is still not uncommon under the disguises of Geillis, Gillia, Julia, Celia, and Cecilia.

Sorcha or Soirge, *bright*, occurs still in the Hebrides, as also in Ulster, but is nearly supplanted in English by the totally unconnected Sarah. It is possible, but unlikely, that Soirge should be the Scandinavian Swerga. If it should be so, it would be a very rare instance of a *female* name brought to the Highlands by the North-men.

Una, thought by some to be Norse, is now rare, but always appears unchanged.

To these must be added Mòr, and its diminutive, Mòrag, a very frequent name, the bearers of which are unaccountably called in English Sarah.

Note 11. Page 17.

The incident here recorded may have suggested to the author of the Lady of the Lake the beautiful passage in Canto V. ix. of that Poem—

" Have then thy wish. He whistled shrill,
And he was answered from the hill," &c.

There is no reason to doubt the derivation of the names of places in Glenlyon referred to in the text from the incidents of this battle ; but whatever be its etymology, the name of Glenlyon itself is of far more ancient date, although it had of old also the descriptive names of Glen-dhui and Glen-fàsach.

Note 12. Page 10.

For two or three centuries the successive Chiefs, Macdougall of Dunolly, Macnachtan of Dundarave, and MacIver of Lergachonzie, no doubt as descended from the same mother, Christina of Craignish, preserved a brotherly intimacy and friendsbip. They are often found associated as witnesses to each others legal transactions, and as acting together on public occasions. See page 24.

Christina of Craignish was unfortunate in being the heiress of the family estates before the country bad become familiarized with the feudal law of succession. Persecuted during life by her uncle and tho male branches of the race, to whom the succcssion of a female appeared unlawful, shc was obliged to purchase support by some concessions of land to powerful neighbours The descendants of the male line, wbo soon afterwards recovered Craignisb, revenged themselves by assailing her memory and that of her husbands, especially Mac-Iver, with ridiculously slanderous legends and foul epithets—the true motive of which was, however, always wcll understood in the country. The author of the Craignisb MS.. referred to in the text, repeats these with relish, as if they had been well-founded ; but, with strange inconsistency, when, some generations afterwards, a representative of the Craignish family marries the only child of a branch of tbe Macdougalls, be complains bitterly that her father's estate, which had been settled on heirs *male,* did not come with ber to the House of Craignish.

Note 13.   Page 22.

In his Life of Thomas Campbell the poet, the amiable author, Dr. Beattie, blindly follows the absurd statement referred to in Note 3 as to the origin of. the Clan given by Robert, the poet's uncle.

The poet himself was no genealogist ; witness the following lines from his otherwise heautiful poem, written on receiving a seal hearing the Campbell (hoar's head) crest in 1817 :

> " So speed my song—mark'd with thc crest
> That erst the adventurous Norman wore,
> Who won the Lady of the West,
> Tbe daughter of Macaillan Mor."

Thc evidence of the Norman descent of the progenitor of the Camphells (notwithstanding the great efforts of the Scannachies, in deference to Highland feeling, to represent the husband of Eva Nic-Dhiarmid O'Duinn as himself a Highlander of her family), has heen shewn above in Note 5. But although the Campbell shield, gyronny of eight *or* and *sable* (formerly *argent* and *sable*), is doubtless of Norman origin, the boar's bead crest was certainly not the cognizance of " the adventurous Norman," hut of Eva's family, " the race of Brown Diarmid who slew the wild hoar." Eva too, " the Lady of the West," instead of being " the daughter of Macaillan Mor," was probably tbe mother or grandmother of Colin the Great, from whom that well-known patronymic of the Heads of the House of Argyll was derived.

The illustrious poet had, bowever, far higher qualities than those of a genealogist. Thc poem from wbich tbe ahove extract is takcn contains some stanzas of great beauty, and his lincs written " On visiting a scene in Argyllshire"—Kirnan, the home of his family—are exquisite at once for pathos and moral grandeur. It will ever be the pride of the Clan-lver to cherish the memory of this gifted member of their race—the author, as pronounced by high autbority, at once of the finest didactic and the finest martial poems in the English language. The writer, who was connected with the poet's family by a nearer tie of relationship than that merely of clansman, rejoices in the possession of some juvenile letters and poems in the poet's handwriting, and also of a copy of the first smaller edition of the Pleasures of Hope, with his autograph, the author's gift to his relative and early friend, the writer's father.

It is unnecessary to say anything here of the poet's family in recent generations, in regard to which the information in Beattie, and in the shorter Lives prefixed to his Works, is sufficiently correct. See Genealogical Tables.

Note 14. Page 22.

Of the ancient baronial mansion of Lergachonzie scarce a vestige remains. It stood on the edge of a low natural terrace on the north side of the high road between the head of Loch-Craignish and Kilmelfort, and was known by the name of *Seòmar bàn Mhic-Imheair*—" Mac-Iver's White Hall." The spot is still designated *Làr an-t-Sheòmair*, or "the Site of the Hall." A few stones that formed part of the building, are pointed out in the walls of the neighbouring cottages, and places are shewn where pipes, that conducted water to the Hall from the neighbouring heights, were dug up.

Note 15. Page 22.

A strange import has been assigned to the privilege of *mercheta mulierum* in this instance. It has been represented as equivalent to a right known as *jus primæ noctis*, and equally misunderstood. The traditional interpretation in the present case is easily accounted for. Before the occupation of Finncharn by the MacIvers, it was the possession of a Chieftain of the Macdonald race, styled Mac-Vic-Iain, who, according to a well-known legend, related in the New Statistical Account of Glassary, endeavoured to enforce in a certain instance the barbarous claim referred to, and drew upon himself a violent death and the destruction of his castle. The story came, as stories often do, to attach to the long subsequent occupants of Finncharn, the MacIvers, and was vulgarly thought to receive authentication from the privilege of *mercheta mulierum* in their title deeds—in ignorance alike of the meaning of that privilege and of its very common occurrence in baronial charters. The author of the Statistical Account, although giving the legend correctly, is wrong in saying that the Castle of Finncharn, when burnt on that occasion, was not built again. The castle destroyed was not that of which the ruins now exist—which was built on the site of the preceding fortalice, in the thirteenth or fourteenth century. For the meaning of *mercheta mulierum*, and of *jus primæ noctis*, see Sir David Dalrymple, Lord Hailes—Annals of Scotland, Appendix I. The former appears to have generally implied a fine payable by a serf or villain, who, by giving his daughter in marriage to the inhabitant of another barony, diminished the number of his lord's subjects.

Note 16. Page 24.

This singular document is here given at length :

In Dei nomine . Amen . Per hoc praesens publicum instrumentum cunctis pateat evidenter et sit notum, quod, anno incarnationis dominicae millesimo quingentesimo sexagesimo quarto, mensis vero Augusti die decimo nono, indictione quarta, in mei notarii publici [et] testium subscriptorum [praesentia.] The quhilk day, in presence of me notar publick, and witnes underwrytten, personalie apperit, ane potent and nobile erle Archibald erle of Argyle, lord Campbell and Lorne, etc. and thair of his awin free motiefe, uncompellit, or coacted yairto, and for spetial cause and favors, and certin soumies of money and othyer goudis payit and dounne to us by our cousin Ever Mak Ever of Lergachonzie, grantis us to haif sauld, disponit, and simpliciter overgiffen : Likeas we, be the tenor of yis present instrument, sellis, disponis, and simpliciter overgiffs to the said Ever Mak Ever of Lergachonzie, his airs and assignayis, and successoris quhatsumever, our ryght, tytle, and kyndnes quhatsumever, we, our predecessoris and successoris hed, his, or any manner of way may claim, haif interes or ryght to, all manner of calpis qubatsumever, aucht and wynt to come to our hous of the surname of Mak Ever in ony times bygane, or aucht to come to our house in tymes comyng, to remain with the said Ever Mak Ever of Lergachonzie, his airs, assignayis, and successoris qubatsumever, heritable for ever, giffand, grantand, turnand, and transferrand, fra us, our airs and successoris, all rygbt, kyndnes, and possessione quhatsumever, of the calpis of the forementioned surname of Clan Ever in and to the said Ever Mak Ever of Lergachonzie, his airis, assignayis, and successoris qubatsumever, with power to him and thaim and thair factoris in all time here-after, to uise, uplift, intromit, and uptake the calpis of the abovenamed surname, quhan thay sall happen to vaik, to thair awin utilitie and profite, and to dispone yairupon as yay sale tbink expedient, as any uther freebalder within our erledome of Ergyle uises he constitutioun ; and sicklike, als freely in ale thyngs as we was wynt to do, and uise of before, providing yat we haif the said Ever's calpe, and his airis and successoris quhatsumever. Super quibus omnibus et singulis dictus Evorus Mak Ever de Lergachonzie de me notario publico subscripto, sibi fieri et dari petiit unum aut plura instrumentum seu instrumenta, publicum aut publica. Acta erant haec apud Dunnoune, hora decima ante meridiem aut eo circa, prae-sentibus ibidem Joanne Campbele de Inverlyver, Colino Camphele de Barbreck, Joanne Campbele de Carrick, Magistro Joanne Bode, Donaldo Campbele Robertson, Archibaldo Campbele de Clachan, cum diversis aliis testibus ad prae-missa vocatis et requisitis. (Follows the docquet :) Ego vero Joannes Lawmount, presbyt. Glasguen. dioces. autoritate apostolica, &c.

Note 17. Page 24.

Sir Robert Douglas's errors—if he is to be held responsible for the latter por-tions of bis work—are too numerous and palpable to be separately pointed out. The various documents relative to tbe MacIvers in the Craignish Charter Cbest, so much referred to as a repository of valuable information by the late Mr. Donald Gregory, of whicb tbe writer has long possessed copies, would have saved Sir Robert from falling into these errors, and now afford the means of so far rectifying them. The records preserved at Inveraray might have been expected to yield further light regarding a family so closely connected with that locality; but there is reason to fear that many documents of the fifteenth and sixteenth centuries existing tbere bad become totally illegible through damp before tbe erection of tbe present castle.

Note 18. Page 25.

The Clan-Gunn had cherished a deadly enmity against the friends of the Countess for some years, in consequence of the execution, by her first husband the Regent Murray, of Alexander the Chief of the Clan at Inverness in 1565.

Note 19. Page 26.

See the character given of Sir Robert Gordon by a friendly judge, Gordon of Sallagh, in the continuation of his History, in which, while Sir Robert is praised for his services to the House of Sutherland, he is admitted to have been " too far transported and carried with a fervent affection that way." " too vehement and passionate in any action." Sallagh, after enumerating his good points, says : " But men are not saints. These virtues must needs be accompanied with some vices ; a bitter enemy as long as he professed it ; and cholerick." In the preface to Sir Robert's Work, dated from Dunrobin Castle, Oct. 1, 1812, regret is expressed for his " hostile feelings concerning others, many of whom were probably equally entitled to complain of aggression on the part of those whom he defends." At page 194 of the History of the House and Clan of Mackay, Gordon is strongly condemned as a sycophant of King James VI., " supple, time-serving, haughty, wrathful, ambitious." The MacIvers may easily endure the vituperation of so prejudiced an author.

The writer of these pages can hardly be suspected of unfairness towards Sir Robert Gordon, who was his ancestor, maternally, in the same degree exactly as William Buey MacIver was on the father's side. Sir Robert Gordon's daughter, Katharine, married David Barclay of Urie, and was mother of the celebrated Apologist for the Quakers, and of Jean Barclay, wife of the famous Sir Ewen Cameron of Lochiel, by whom she had, with other children, Lucy, who married Peter Campbell of Barcaldine.

Note 20. Page 27.

The practice of designating the successive representatives of a family by an epithet originally descriptive, but which had ceased to be personally applicable, was not unknown in Scotland. In Ireland it appears in such designations as Macnamara Finn (white) and Macnamara Reach (swarthy) ; O'Kennedy Finn, O'Kennedy Roe (red), and O'Kennedy Don (brown) ; O'Farrell Bayne (fair) and O'Farrell Buey (yellow-haired), written often Boy ; and it still subsists in the familiar titles of O'Connor Don and O'Connor Roe. In Scotland we have a well known instance in the case of the Robertsons Roy, *Scotice* Reid, of Straloch, who eventually adopted Reid as their sole surname. Of this family, the last was General Reid, who founded the Chair of Music in the University of Edinburgh.

Note 21. Page 28.

Gordon calls William's son-in-law " Gilcolm M'Soirl." He was of the family of Lamont of Monydrain, or Monydrynan, in Glassary, called patronymically Mac-Shomhairleadh, (sometimes written as pronounced, M'Coirl), from its progenitor, Somerled Lamont. The property, though much diminished, has continued till the present year in possession of the Lamonts, and a receipt in the writer's hands shews that some documents relative to part of the estate were even at the middle of the last century in the keeping of William Buey's descendants. Gordon also calls Gilcolm " ane islander"—most probably as connected with and occasionally living in Tiree. The Argyll family having some time previously got possession of a portion of that island, of which they afterwards became the sole proprietors, had induced many of their friends and allies from the mainland to settle there.   Among these were some of the Lamonts, of whom the Lamonts of Monydrain were then a leading family. The name Lamout is even yet not unfrequent in Tiree.

Some of the Mackinvin sept of the Maclachlans are still to be met with. One of them was landlord of the Inn at Kilmichael-Glassary about twenty years ago.

Although, in one place, Gordon speaks in a loose way of Caithness as William Buey's " native soil," there is every reason for believing that he was born in Argyllshire, and that, being an infant at the time of his father's removal to the North, he had been left behind till of sufficient age to have become well known there. Apart from his own distinct statement that he had " originallie come out of Argyll," the readiness and zeal with which his cause is espoused by Lord Lorne, the marriage of his daughter in Argyllshire, and the wonderful influence he exerts over his clansmen and relatives in that county, in inducing them to follow him for several successive years in his perilous enterprises, can hardly be explained on the mere ground of his near relationship to the Chiefs of the Clan, without supposing him also to have been, before these events, personally well known in Argyllshire, and to have maintained communication with his friends there.

The names of all William Bney's sons and grandsons have not been recovered. It seems certain, however, that he had two sons besides the one who perished with him, and that the eldest survivor, the father of Patrick of Quoycrook, Farquhar of Rumsdale, and Alexander of Comelfiet, was named Donald ; and as there appears no room to doubt the identity of this Donald with " Donald Mac-William-Mac-Iver" mentioned on page 30, it follows that the " John Mac-William-Mac-Iver" mentioned along with him was, most probably, his brother. There are reasons for supposing that there was a third surviving son, but, if so, his name is lost.

Note 22. Page 29.

The form Iverach is analogous to Griogarach, Dughallach, Domhnullach, Mathanach, Cattanach, Allanach, for McGregor, McDougall, &c. The forms bear to each other much the same relation as would Ivericus and Iverides. The name Iverach might be applied in a familiar or colloquial manner to any member of the Clan. The family by which it has been permanently adopted as a surname, appear about two centuries ago for some generations under that name in possession of Brachour, in the parish of Halkirk, and also as tenants of importance at Liurary and other places in the neighbourhood. It is respectably represented in Orkney by Mr. Iverach of Wideford, near Kirkwall.

Note 23. Page 33.

After the victory, the Earl appointed Finlay his own Piper, and adopted the air so happily extemporized by him as " Breadalbane's March." The words,

Bodaich-na-briogais, " Bodies wi' the breeks," are descriptive of the Sinclairs, who wore the low-country dress, their adversaries the Campbells and MacIvers being clad in the Highland garb. Calder, in his History of Caithness, represents Finlay as a native of Perthshire. He was more probably the son of a Finlay MacIver, who lived at Stainland, in the Parish of Thurso, and he continued to reside in Caithness for a considerable time after the battle of Altimarlach, although perhaps he may have removed to Perthshire ultimately, with Lord Breadalbane. His Chief, Campbell of Quoycrook, seems to have shewn his sense of the gallant piper's merit by becoming godfather, *goisteadh,* at ·the baptism of his son Alexander, in 1687. Among Calder's mistakes in regard to Finlay, may be mentioned his ascribing to him the authorship of the " *Campbells are coming*" and of " *Failt Chlann-Imheair.*" See below, Note 29.

Note 24. Page 34.

William Roy Campbell, or MacIver, is sometimes named, from his father, MacFarquhar—in Gaelic *MacFhearchair*—whence he is called in some writings MacKerchar and MacKyrchar. After the death of his uncle and father-in-law, Quoycrook, and in the absence of his cousin, the Reverend Donald or Daniel Campbell, he acted as the head of the MacIvers in Caithness. He was long remembered for his genial disposition and profuse hospitality. It is related that on one occasion the Chief of the Gunns, attended by the usual following, paid William Roy a formal visit at Rumsdale. To bury the remembrance of rencounters of a very different kind on the part of their forefathers, William Roy, with the rude hospitality of the day, broached an anker of brandy. After three days spent in festivity, the whole party set out on foot to pay a visit to Mackay of Bighouse, twenty miles distant, a gillie of William's carrying the anker on his shoulder. On reaching the top of Knocksletil, about half way to Bighouse, they stopped to refresh themselves, and the anker having been emptied, William gave it a kick, on which it rolled to the foot of the hill, and half-a-mile along the level. For this anecdote the writer is indebted to Captain Gunn of Braehour, a descendant of the Chiefs of the Clan-Gunn in Caithness.

Note 25. Page 34.

Some of his relatives, Campbells from Perthshire, followed Glenorchy on his first arrival in Caithness in 1669, and as he quartered some of his troops in the county for three or four years after 1680, a few more Perthshire Campbells may have remained behind. But almost all these are understood to have withdrawn from Caithness when Glenorchy disposed of his property there.

There are also in Caithness some Campbells said to be descended from a family which came into Caithness through Tongue, in Sutherland, about 130 years ago, and settled at Achavarasdale, in the Caithness part of Reay, now the property of Sir Robert Sinclair of Stevenston and Murkle.

None of these are to be confounded with the Campbells of the Clan-Iver.

Note 26. Page 34.

Accounts still exist of payments to Patrick Campbell of Quoycrook, for supplies purchased by him for Breadalbane's troops, stationed in the west of

Caithness, probably at Castle Braal, down to 1684, under the command of the Honourable John Campbell, the Earl's son, afterwards second Earl of Breadalbane.

Among his other qualities, Patrick Campbell possessed a talent for the composition of Gaelic verse. One of his productions was a poem on the frost of August 1694, which occasioned a famine in Caithness. Of this poem two stanzas have been preserved by the author of the Old Statistical Account, whose Gaelic spelling, however, and translation into English, it has been found necessary to replace as follows :

An reodha thainig air dia-domhnaich,
Chuir e bròn a's mulad orm ;
Choisg e mise o'n òl,
'S nithe mòr cha b'fhurasd leam.

Ged churainn ceithir fhear a bhualadh,
Cheart cho cruaidh 's a b'urradh dhoibh ;
Nuair a sguabadh leo an làr,
Cha dheanamh e tradh do'n mhuirichinn.

Woe's me ! That fatal Sunday's frost
Hath wrought me dule and care,
Left dry my cheerful cup, and blown
All my fine schemes to air.

Four of my stoutest hinds all day
With might the flail may ply ;
The floor at evening swept will scarce
One scanty meal supply.

Several proofs appear of the continued regard of the Breadalbane family towards that of Patrick Bucy. It may be mentioned that on the death of his grandson, the Rev. James Campbell of Duchernan, Minister of Kilbrandon, in 1742, Colin Campbell of Carwhin—a near relative of Lord Breadalbane, whose son succeeded as fourth Earl—then resident as the Earl's Factor at Ardmaddy Castle, and who had been Mr. Campbell's intimate and attached friend, voluntarily undertook the management of the affairs of the widow and family. Some family papers in his hand-writing still exist to show his activity and kindness.

Note 27. Page 34.

Murdoch Campbell, Quoycrook's son-in-law, was the son of William—styled "Beag" or "the Little"—who may have been a cousin-german of Quoycrook's, and a son of John-Mac-William-MacIver. Murdoch appears to have been the same who afterwards possessed the lands of Tofthorsa, and is sometimes designated from them. To him his mother in law made over her life-interest in a portion of the Quoycrook property. He was probably the grand-father of Murdoch Campbell, writer in Thurso about the middle of last century.

Quoycrook—it ought to have been stated sooner—has been for a century and a half called Quarrycrook, a name more in accordance with the etymology, which is undoubtedly *coire, car,* or *cor-a-chruic.* The name has no connection whatever with the *quoy* of Orkney and Shetland, which, although found in a very few instances on the main-land, forms there the last, not the first, part of

the words in which it occurs. Almost all the names of places in the immediate neighbourhood are of Gaelic origin, and a stream near the spot is called *alt-a-choire*. The form Quoycrook has, however, been retained in this work as that which occurs in the charters and old documents in the author's possession, and as that by which the family was best known, although sometimes designated of Calder—Scots-Calder—in the neighbourhood. The form most in accordance with analogy would probably be *Corrycrook*.

Note 28. Page 35.

The following is the Testimonial mentioned in the text :

Omnibus et singulis cujuscunque ordinis status seu dignitatis in rei sive politicæ sive ecclesiasticæ administratione constitutis, ad quorum manus hæc pervenerint, fausta omnia et prospera a Deo O. M. comprecamur. Cbyrographis nostris subscriptis notum facimus præsentium Latorem Magistrum Danielem Campbell Scoto-Britannum Cathanensem, parentibus undiquaque laudatissimis et fide dignis in hac nostra parochia in legittimo conjugio prognatum, Juvenem esse probum ingenuum et excultum, atque ab ineunte ætate apud nos illibatam egisse vitam ; Qui, post liberalem et ingenuam in literis humanioribus eruditionem, in Inclyta Universitate Regia Aberdonensi curriculum quadriennale summa cum Doctorum laude feliciter evolvit; ubi rerum philosophicarum artiumque liberalium notitiam ita assecutus est, ut ab omnibus præ animi candore, morum gravitate, vitæ integritate, ac ingenii cultura, summam consequutus sit benevolentiam. Quocirca cum candido ac plurimo dilecto juveni in votis sit, ad uberiorem ingenii culturam, Exteras regiones Externorumque mores ac cultus quantum fieri poterit perlustrare ; Illum omnibus virtutum fautoribus ubivis gentium literis hisce nostris commendititiis amice commendamus, obnixe rogantes ut ab omnibus apud quos peregrinatus fuerit, omni qua par est benevolentia et amore accipiatur, prout suos a nobis prosequi velint . His datis apud Thurso 15to die mensis Maii A.D. Millesimo sexcentesimo octuagesimo septimo muniendis ac attestandis unanimiter coeunt:

And : Cathanen ;
Joannes Sylvius, Pastor
Joannes Fortoune
R (?) Boynd, Balivus de Thurso
Gulielmus Younger
Gullielmus Munro

Gull. Sinclair, Cathanen.
Commissarius.
Joa : Macphersonus, Ses. Cls.
D. Harper, Nórius Publicus.
Joannes Murravius, Nuper Balivus de Thurso.

In a MS. of a few pages, the beg ning of an autobiography by the Rev. Daniel Campbell, which the writer oft.n read over in his boyhood, but which were long ago lost sight of during his absence from Britain, Daniel recorded that he "was born at Quoycrook on Lammas-day, 1665, being the son of Patrick Campbell of Quoycrook, descendit of the Black Knichts of Lochow, and of Helen Bayne or Mackay, descendit of my Lord Reay." The narrative mentioned his having been, when a very little boy, during a visit to his uncle at Rumsdale, nearly killed by a gander, who bit a piece out of his naked thigh, —an injury of which he bore the marks during life—and left off after a touching allusion to the death of the companion adverted to in the text. and to a vision which he had had in a state of feverishness resulting from sleeplessness and grief

after that event, and which seems to have made a deep and permanent impression on him.

Although he appears to have been unwilling to enter the ranks of the existing
Church Establishment in Scotland, under which his kinsmen in Argyllshire had
suffered so sorely, he seems to have had no objections to Episcopacy, and even
to have had some intention of entering the Church of England when he left his
home in 1687. His mind was too deeply impressed with matters of vital importance, too serious and practically earnest, to attach much importance to forms
of ecclesiastical polity.

Note 29. Page 35.

Of 42 signers of the Call to Mr. Daniel Campbell to be Minister of Glassary,
Sept. 29, 1691, 22 are Campbells, among whom are Sir Duncan Campbell of
Auchinbreck, and Campbell of Barbreck, the majority of the others being pro-
bably MacIvers. Of the remaining 20 signers, five are Maclachlans, and four
Lamonts.

While there are many reasons for believing that Daniel Campbell was present at the battle of Altimarlach, his extreme youth can scarcely be an argument
against his having been so. As the well-grown son of a chief, he could hardly
have been absent, and a tradition still exists that he had been a soldier in early
life, and that some of his parishioners had first seen him arrayed in the Highland
garb, and brandishing a broadsword. One of his descendants in the fifth generation, Lorne Colin Campbell, third son of Dr. Duncan Campbell of Toronto, the
writer's brother, was present as a member of the Queen's Own Volunteer Rifle
Regiment about the same age—fifteen and four months—in the action of Ridge-
way in Canada, against the Fenians, on the 2nd June, 1866. Seven of his
Company, one of two ordered to the front on the unexpected appearance of the
Fenians, were killed or mortally wounded—one of them, a corporal, who stood
next to him, being shot through the head at his side.

Note 30. Page 36.

As a proof of the esteem in which Mr. Campbell was held in the Church, it
may be mentioned that having been appointed, immediately after his induction,
Clerk of the Presbytery of Inverary, he was in the following year chosen Mode-
rator of the Synod of Argyll, and, on retiring from the Chair, Synod-Clerk, an
appointment which he held till induced by ill-health to resign it in 1708. But
the most difficult and honourable post assigned to him. and one which incontes-
tably proves the reliance placed on his wisdom and influence, was that of Mode-
rator of the Commission of Visitation of Synod appointed to visit the whole
bounds, for the purpose of deposing incumbents who obstinately refused to submit
to the Presbyterian Church Government, and receiving the submission of those
who conformed, as well as to report on such measures as might seem advisable for
restoring the discipline of the Church. This delicate duty he discharged with
great faithfulness and dignity, and at the same time with such wisdom, tender-
ness, and success. that, with hardly an exception, the Episcopal Clergy of
Argyllshire soon cordially coalesced with their Presbyterian brethren in carrying
on the work of the Church, some of the more eminent of them contracting with

Mr. Campbell friendships which ended only with life, and transmitting to their descendants a warm and respectful regard for his memory. Among these was the Rev. Colin Campbell of Achnaba, (of the Barcaldine family), Minister of Ardchattan, an eminent mathematician, and correspondent of Sir Isaac Newton.

A full list of the Rev. D. Campbell's published Works is given in "Notes and Queries," 3rd Series, vi. 171, 172.

Jean Campbell, the wife of the Rev. Daniel Campbell, was a woman of much energy and presence of mind. Her father, the Rev. Patrick Campbell of Tor blaren, Minister of Inveraray and Glenaray, and his brother, the Rev. Duncan Campbell of Barcuil, Minister of Glenorchy, were "outed" for non-conformity in 1662, but both survived the Revolution,—when the former was replaced, and the latter became Minister of Knapdale. After the unfortunate rising of 1685, Sir Duncan Campbell of Auchinbreck, her father's cousin, who had acted as Argyll's second in command, having been obliged to fly to the Continent, his wife, the excellent Lady Henrietta Lindsay, daughter of the Earl of Balcarras, proceeded to join him, taking with her as a companion her husband's young relative, Jean Campbell, with a view to her being educated in Holland. They were arrested on their way to embark, on suspicion of being the bearers of communications to the friends of Argyll. The suspicion was not unfounded, Lady Henrietta having on her person a letter, which might have proved prejudicial to the Earl or to others, then awaiting their trial. This letter she passed to her companion, while herself awaiting examination. The young lady contrived to tear the letter into small pieces in her pocket, which she chewed and swallowed. In Holland, where the refugees were kindly received at court, Lady Henrietta and Miss Campbell became acquainted with the Princess—afterwards Queen— Anne, then residing with her sister, the Princess of Orange ; and when. after the Revolution, on their return to Scotland, they visited the Princess in London, she presented Lady Henrietta with a shawl as a token of remembrance, and Miss Campbell with a muslin apron, said to have been embroidered by herself. This royal relic is in the writer's possession, to whom it has descended as the great-great-grandson and representative of the lady who received it.

Note 31. Page 38.

The services of Mr. Campbell may be estimated from a simple enumeration of the ships in which he served successively as Midshipman, Mate, and Lieutenant—the Dido, Téméraire, Latona, Victor, Kent, Ruby, Saturn, Royal Oak, Terrible, Dreadnought. When obliged by the state of his health to retire from the sea, before receiving the promotion which he had so well earned, he held for a time the appointment of Commander of Sea-Fencibles for the Leith District.

Note 32. Page 43.

Robert Campbell was enabled to pay for his purchases of land, partly by his wife's fortune, and partly by his uncle, Alexander of Kilbride, who was reluctantly persuaded to advance to Robert a large portion of his savings by their relative, Campbell of Ardlarach. Robert executed an entail of all his property, inherited and acquired—failing his own issue and that of his brothers and sisters— on connections of his English wife, of the names of Yates, Ashton, Nooth,

Vavasour, &c., requiting the services of Ardlarach, who was, moreover, his own next relative on the female side, with the empty honour of being named after all these English families.

Note 33. Page 44,

It seems right to record here the circumstances in which this claim was formally made.

When, in 1853, Mr. Paterson, through the extinction of all the prior heirs of tailzie, came into possession of the property entailed by Robert Campbell of Ashnish, an anonymous paragraph appeared in an Edinburgh newspaper, intimating that he had obtained from the Lyon-Depute licence to use the name and arms of Campbell and MacIver, and so worded as to convey the impression that he had thus become the *Chief of the Clan-Iver !* A claim so extraordinary as that of an individual to have become the head of a race of which he was not even a member, might, it may perhaps be thought, have been left unnoticed. But, while it seemed possible that such a claim, however valueless in the eyes of the well informed, might gain some sort of popular credit, it also appeared on other grounds, obligatory on the writer not to allow it to remain uncontradicted. Accordingly, his agent, W. P. Allardice, Esq., W.S., at that time a member of one of the first provincial firms in Scotland, published a letter with his signature, in reference to the paragraph in question, explaining the true state of the case ; while the writer himself communicated with the Lyon-Depute, requesting that the grant of licence to Mr. Paterson to use the name and arms of Campbell and MacIver, as a condition of holding the entailed property, might be so guarded as in no way to prejudice the rights of the heir male as Head of the Clan, or to countenance any pretension of Mr. Paterson (now Duncan MacIver Campbell) to that position ; and, in particular, that the use of the Supporters, the special armorial distinction of the Chiefs, should be withheld from him. The Lyon-Depute, in reply, assured the writer that the licence to Mr. Paterson in no way interfered with the rights of the heir male, and that the Supporters, which Mr. Paterson had applied for, had been refused to him.

Presuming, however, on the supposed ignorance of the public and the members of the Clan in regard to this and the other facts of the case, Mr. Paterson endeavoured to counteract the statement of the writer's agent by irrelevant personalities and insidious misrepresentations, of which it is enough here to say that an influential journal, which had inadvertently admitted them into its columns (after they had been refused by another), expressed in a subsequent number its deep regret for having done so, apologizing to the writer and his agent, and justifying the position assumed by them, in the most ample and satisfactory terms. The circumstances having thus become sufficiently known, it seemed unnecessary to take serious notice of any further attempts which Mr. Paterson or MacIver Campbell might make to obtain acceptance for his claim.

Although the position of representative of an ancient and honourable family, when dissevered from its inheritance, may seem to some in these days scarce worthy of being maintained, yet the writer's interposition on the occasion above mentioned, although competent to any member of the Clan, appeared to lay him under an obligation to shew some special right on his own part to interfere.

Accordingly, acting under the advice of Counsel, he formally preferred, in the Court of the Lord Lyon, his own claim as the heir male and representative of the MacIvers of Lergachonzie, Stronshiray, and Asknish; and although—from the difficulty and the expense—a serious matter where no property is at stake—of establishing, *in legal shape*, remote links of filiation—the formal proof has not yet been completed, he has the satisfaction of having preserved from an attempted usurpation, on behalf of his own family, or of any other *member of the Branch* who may shew a preferable claim, the representation of the very old and interesting race from which they are descended.

This is not a fit place for setting forth the genealogical proofs of the writer's claim, but, both in explanation of his interference on the above-mentioned occasion, and as a presumptive evidence of his right, the following circumstances may be recorded.

Soon after the death, in 1818, of Sir Trafford Campbell, the last of the direct line of Asknish, his widow, passing through Glasgow—with the intention of proceeding to Wales—while in the house of Mrs Campbell, widow of the Rev. George Campbell of Ardchattan, (of the Quoycrook or Duchernan Family), the fellow-student and intimate friend of Sir Trafford, delivered to Mrs. Campbell, along with Sir Trafford's watch, the armorial seal used by the Family of Asknish, as Chiefs of the Clan-Iver, " to be kept," as stated in a declaration by Mrs. Campbell, " for her eldest son"—the present writer—" then a boy at school, as an undoubted descendant of the said Family in the male line, than whom none nearer to the said Sir Trafford was known to her. the said Lady Campbell.''

In this act, Lady Campbell, who was devotedly attached to her husband. (to whom it was her great grief not to have borne an heir), and much interested in his relation to the Clan, must be reasonably presumed to have proceeded under an impression received from him, that on the extinction—by his death without male issue—of the direct line of Asknish, the Family of Quoycrook and Duchernan, although it had struck off at a remote period, became probably the representative of the Lergachonzie Branch, its descent from which was never questioned or doubted.

Lady Campbell was unable from illness to proceed farther than Glasgow, and died there after a confinement of about nine months, in May 1819. In her will, drawn up six months before her death, the gift of the watch, made about the same time, to Mrs. Campbell, was found specially mentioned as a bequest, destined for the family of Mrs. Campbell's husband, "*who are MacIvers, very few of the Branch remaining.*"

The writer naturally felt bound, on attaining manhood, to enquire into the subject—prepared, as he has ever been, on discovering the existence of any member of the [Lergachonzie] Branch nearer than himself, cheerfully to acknowledge the right of such person to the Chieftainship of the Clan, and to the armorial seal in his keeping. But he has failed, after years of inquiry, to discover any such person or any one even claiming to be such. All the circumstances now mentioned, and the result of these investigations, were fully known to the last surviving sister of Sir Trafford, Mrs. Jekyll, then Campbell of Asknish,

K

were communicated by her, at the writer's desire, to her legal agents, and were never called in question.*

Note 34. Page 45.

The song referred to is said to have been composed by the Piper in an inn in Kunpdale, when his pipe was seized by the hostess for non-payment of his score. The song and story were carried by the MacIvers to the north, and Calder, in his work on Caithness, places the scene of the anecdote and the origin of the tune in that county. The tune, however, is much older than the song, and the song than the expedition to Caithness. Its local allusions fix the place of its composition. Of this effusion, the following somewhat unconnected stanzas have been preserved :

> Thoir dhomh mo phìoh, a's theid mi dhachaidh,
> 'S mur faidh mi ì, chadh d' theid mi dhachaidh ;
> Ged a dhòluinn togaid fhìon,
> Chadh dhiultadb a phaidheadh Clann Imhear Ghlasraith.

> Mhic 'Ilebhearnaig† n'an cuil crìon,
> Nuair thig an Righ, theid cuir as duit ;
> Thoir dhomh &c

> Nuair ruigeas sinn tràigh a Chrionain.
> Seinnidh siu pìob, a's theid sinn dachaidh ;
> Thoir dhomh &c.

> Seinuidh sinn pìob, a's theid siun dachaidh,
> Gu tigh mòr au urlar fharsaing ; ‡
> Thoir dhomh &c.

Note 35. Page 46.

As each Clan had its bonnet badge—generally some plant characteristic of its territory—so, in many cases, birds and other animals were regarded as allied to, or symbolical of, particular races or confederations in the Highlands. Thus, the magpie was considered friendly to the Campbells, perhaps for no better reason than its wearing the old Campbell colours, *argent* and *sable*, changed in the sixteenth century to *or* and *sable*. In like manner the horse was a symbol or friend of the MacIvers of Glassary. The following piece of Gaelic folk-lore was often heard by the writer in his boyhood :—

> Crodh maol Chnapdail,
> Eich chlòimheach Ghlasraith,
> Fitlich dhubh Chraiginnis,
> 'S Coilich Airisceodnis.

---

* Iu 1870, Mr. Paterson, having again changed his name to Dnncan Campbell MacIver, printed and circulated privately, under the title of " Remarks, &c.," a strange attack on the author of these pages. These " Remarks" may be left safely to the judgment of those who may have seen them. But a few copies still remain of an answer by the author's Agent, Mr. Allardice, and can be had on application by any person who may have received Mr. Duncan Campbell MacIver's " Remarks."

† M'Ilvernock of Obe. a small proprietor in North Knapdale, who would appear to have taken part against the piper on the occasion.

‡ Probably MacIver's *Seòmar làn*

The polled oxen of Knapdale,
The shaggy horses of Glassary,
The black ravens of Craignish,
And the cocks of Ariskeodnish.

The horse was also a symbol of the MacDougalls.

Note 36. Page 49.

The heraldic dictionaries give two MacIver coats as borne in England. 1, M'Iver (Liverpool): Quarterly or and gules, a bend azure. Crest: A boar's head couped or. Motto: *Nunquam obliviscar.* 2, M'Iver (England): Quarterly (parti-per-cross) or and gules, on a bend sable. three mullets or. Crest: A griffin's head erased azure.

These arms may perhaps have some sanction from the Herald's College of England. But it is to be regretted, for their own sakes, that members of Scottish families should commit the mistake of seeking authority for armorial bearings in England and Ireland, instead of applying to the Court of the Lord Lyon, the only authority in Scottish heraldry. The sanction of the Lord Lyon would be a genealogical record of real value, and serious errors would be avoided, which often appear in the arms borne by descendants of Scottish families in the other parts of the United Kingdom.

Sketch of the Genealogy of the Family of Lergachonzie, Stronshiray, or Asknish, Chiefs of the Clan-Iver, from Iver MacIver of Lergachonzie, the Chief in 1565, supposed to have been the 13th in succession from Iver the Progenitor of the race, and the 10th Baron of Lergachonzie.

I. IVER, 1565

DUNCAN, d. s. p.

CHARLES, of Stronshiray, supposed to have died v. p. and to have md. a dr. of Kenneth M'Lachlan of Kellenochanach.

IVER BAYNE, feuar of Lergachonzie—his issue extinct in the third generation.

II. DUNCAN (Sir) of Stronshiray and Lergachonzie, md. 1st, Katharine Campbell, supposed a dr. of Dunstaffnage, 2nd, a dr. of Somerled Buey Macdonald, and sister of first Earl of Antrim.

KENNETH BUEY, progenitor of Quoyerook and Ducherman, Chief of the Clan-Iver in Caithness, 1589-1616.

FARQUHAR, killed at Pollhour, 1594.

IVER, died in his father's lifetime, before 1602.

III. CHARLES, of Asknish, succeeded his Nephew, Iver Og, before 1606.

MARY, md. Ronald Campbell of Barchbeyan, by whom she had John of Craignish and Farquhar of Laganlochan, &c

II. IVER (Og, died s. p. before 1606.

ANGUS, heir apparent in 1612, d s p.

IV. IVER, forfeited 1685; his son, Duncan, restored 1689.

V. DUNCAN, md. — MacAlister, dr. of MacA. of Loup.

VI. DUNCAN, d. s. p.

VII. ANGUS, md. Catharine, dr. of Campbell of Dunstaffnage.

MALCOLM. d. s. p.

DONALD, d. s. p.

A Daughter md. Neil Campbell of Ardlarach, and had issue.

VIII. ANGUS. md. Elizabeth, dr of John M'Lachlan of Craiganterve.

DUNCAN, Collector of Excise in Glasgow, d. s. p. 1797.

ARCHIBALD, Midshipman, R.N. d. s. p.

ALEXANDER, d s. p.

ANGUS, perished at sea, 1755, s. p.

JAMES, R.M. d. s. p.

ALEXANDER, d s. p. Alasdair dubh Chilbride.

AGNES, md. Walter Paterson, and had issue.
SUSAN, md. Rev. Hugh Campbell, d. s. p.
CATHARINE, md. — Leiteh, issue believed extinct.
ISABEL, md. Duncan Campbell of Eskart, and had issue.

IX. ROBERT, Sheriff of Argyll, md. Catharine-Eleanora, dr. of Mall Yates of Maghull, Co. Lancaster.

ELIZABETH HARRIETT, d. unmd.
CATHARINE-ELEANOR, md. Capt. Hamilton, d. s. p.
SARAH CHARLOTTE, md. Nathaniel Jekyll, Capt. 43rd Reg., d. s. p.

X. Sir HORNBURY TRAFFORD, Convener and Sheriff of Argyll, md. Elizth., dr. of John Williams of Ruthyn, Co. Denbigh, d. s. p. 1818.

ℑ. ᴅɪʀᴇᴄᴛ ᴄᴀᴅᴇᴛs ᴏꜰ ᴛʜᴇ ʟᴇʀɢᴀᴄʜᴏɴᴢɪᴇ ʙʀᴀɴᴄʜ.

I. The MacIVERS BUEY or CAMPBELLS of *Quoycrook* and *Calder (Scots-Calder)*, in *Caithness*, afterwards of *Duchernan*, in the County of *Argyll*, Chiefs of the Clan-Iver in Caithness :

I. Kenneth MacIver, styled *Buey* or *Yellow-haired*, Chief of the Clan-Iver in Caithness (see pp. 24, 25), had two sons who attained manhood :
  1. William Buey, his successor.
  2. John, from whom are supposed to have descended the elder family of the Campbells of *Thurso*, afterwards of *Castlehill* and *Lochend*, in Caithness.—See below.

II. William Buey MacIver, afterwards Campbell, sometimes called, from his Father, MacKenneth or Kennethson, whose history is given in pages 27-29, had at least three sons ;
  1. A son, name unknown, but probably Kenneth, who was put to death, when young, with his Father, and died unmarried.
  2. Donald, who continued the line.
  3. John, supposed the progenitor of the Campbells of Dorary, Brubster, Tofthorsa, Braalbyne, and perhaps also of Brachour and Shurary, although some of these families may be descended from another younger son, of this or a previous generation.

III. Donald Buey, supposed to be the "Donald Mac-William-MacIver," mentioned as at Achness in 1665, had three surviving sons :
  1. Patrick Buey Campbell of Quoycrook, of whom below.
  2. Farquhar of Rumsdale, who, living in the Highland part of the country, was generally known by the old surname MacIver, which appears on his tombstone at Halkirk.* He left a son, William MacIver or Campbell, called William Roy, and sometimes MacFarquhar or MacKerchar, who married Anna, daughter of his uncle, Patrick Campbell of Quoycrook (contract dated 3rd February, 1689), and in the absence of his cousin and brother-in-law, Donald or Daniel Buey—settled as a Clergyman in Argyllshire—acted in the old age and after the death of his father-in-law, as the head of the Clan in Caithness.
  3. Alexander Campbell of Comelfiet or Comlicfoot. He married Agnes Charlieson or Campbell, of the Argyll and Perthshire branch of the Craignish family, known as the Clan-Chearlaich. Alexander died, as his tombstone at Halkirk bears, 10th Nov., 1693,† leaving :
    1. Donald Campbell of Aimster, Chamberlain of Caithness 1690-1703. He died in or before 1713, having had issue,

---

* Here lies the body of an honest gentleman, called Farquhar MacIver, who departed this life . . . . . 1691.

† Here lyes Alexander Campbell of Comelfiet, who died 10th November, 1693.

who are supposed to have died young : 1, Alexander ; 2,
William, b. 1703; 3, Margaret, b. Oct. 1, 1701 :
Katharine, b. 1704.

2. John, who succeeded his father in Comliefoot

3. Isabella, married in 1700, to George Davidson in Bukkies,
of the family of Achangills, heritable Commissary-
Clerks of Caithness, and had issue, of whom descendants
still exist.

IV. Patrick Buey Campbell of Quoycrook—see pages 30-34   Of his
many daughters by his wife, Helen Bayne, of the family of Clyth
or Bilbster, one married Murdoch Campbell in Brubster, afterwards of Tofthorsa, and from them is supposed to have descended
Murdoch Campbell, writer in Thurso in 1750. Another, Anna,
married, February 1689, her cousin-german, William Roy Campbell,
son of her uncle, Farquhar of Rumsdale.

Patrick, dying in 1705, was succeeded by his only son :

V. Donald or Daniel Campbell (the Reverend) of Duchernan and Quoycrook, called in Caithness Donald Buey, in Argyllshire Donald
Mòr. For particulars regarding this excellent and eminent man, see
pages 34-36. He m. 1692, Jean Campbell, daughter of the Rev.
Patrick Campbell of Torblaren, of the Auchinbreck family, by whom
he had one son and five daughters who outlived infancy :

1. James, born 1803, of whom below.

1. Henrietta, b. 1693, m. 1st, 1712, the Rev. Duncan Campbell,
Minister of Kilchrenan, afterwards of Kilmartin (brother of
Campbell of Raschoillie, of the Kilmartin family), who d. 3rd
September, 1736, by whom she had three children, who d. in
infancy. 2ndly, 1741, James Buchanan, son of Buchanan of
Glens, by whom she had no issue. She d. 20th Dec 1762.

2. Helen, m. 23rd December, 1718, the Rev. Patrick Pollock,
Minister of South Knapdale, who d. 1761, and had one
daughter, who d. young. Mrs. Pollock d. 1768

3. Jean, m. 1719, Donald M'Gilchrist, Writer, of the family of
North-Barr, and had issue. The last descendant of this
Branch of the M'Gilchrists, a Naval Officer, is said to have
perished in the Royal George, off Spithead, 1782.

4. Anne, m. 1734, John M'Alister, Surgeon, but d. without surviving issue

5. Janet, m. 1739, George Macfarlane of Glenralloch, and had
issue, which became extinct on the death, in 1839, of her grandson, George Macfarlane, Esq. of Glenralloch Advocate.

The Rev. Donald or Daniel Campbell, dying March 28th, 1722,
was succeeded by his only son :

VI. James Campbell of Duchernan (the Rev.), Minister of Kilbrandon
and Kilchattan, 1726, m. his cousin Janet, daughter of his uncle

Dugald Campbell, Esq. of Kilmory (she was b. 1703, d. 6th Feb. 1765), and had issue :

1. Duncan, b. 1734, who succeeded, but d. unmarried.
2. Peter (the Rev.), Minister of Kilmichael-Glassary, who continued the line.

1. Helen, d. unmarried at Kilmory, Nov. 1802.
2. Henrietta, d. at Greenock, August, 1812. She m. Captain John M'Kinnon, who died of the effect of wounds received in the American War, leaving: 1, John, writer in Greenock, who m. Janet, daughter of John Carmichael, Esq. of Greenbank, but d. s. p. 1819; 2, James, in the Army, perished at sea. She was buried at Kilmory.
3. Elizabeth, b. 1742. died unmarried at Craignish, 15th Feb. 1830, well known as "Miss Betty Kilmory,"* and as the great depositary of the Caithness traditions of the family.

The Rev. James Campbell of Duchernan died on the 30th or 31st December, 1742, and was succeeded by his elder son :

VII. Duncan Campbell of Duchernan (see page 37), who died unmarried in Jamaica, 2nd September, 1800, and was succeeded by the eldest surviving son of his brother, the Rev. Peter Campbell, to whom we revert.

The Rev. Peter Campbell, Minister of Kilmichael-Glassary, b. 1739, d. 1779 (see page 37), had by his wife, Margaret Scott, the following children :

1. John, b. 23rd April, 1766, Merchant in Virginia, served heir to his father 26th June, 1792, d. unmarried in December 1796.
2. James, of whom below.
3. George, of whom also below.
4. Duncan, b. 12th May, 1770, d. unmarried in Jamaica, Jan. 1797.
5. Archibald, b. 9th June. 1773. d. 27th March, 1774.
6. Peter, b 15th September 1775, d. unmarried in Jamaica, 6th November, 1795.
7. Colin, M.D., Edinburgh, b. July, 1777, d. unmarried at Kingston, Jamaica 8th May, 1824.
8. Donald, b. July, 1778, d. in infancy.
9. Dugald-William, posthumous, b. 6th June, 1779. Merchant at Buenos-Ayres and Babia, d. at Bahia unmarried, 11th July, 1823.

---

* Dugald Campbell of Kilmory had been induced by his brother, Colonel John Campbell of Blackriver. Jamaica, to send all his sons to that colony, with all the means with which he could furnish them, including a loan of the dower of his daughter Janet, Mrs Campbell of Duchernan. At the early death of her husband in 1742, her dower not having been paid, and there being no comfortable house at Duchernan, she obtained, in lieu of it, possession of the house and home-farm of Kilmory, which were occupied by her, and after her by her unmarried daughters, from 1743 till 1805, for a period of 62 years. Her second son, the Rev. Peter Campbell, lived also with her at Kilmory during the first years of his incumbency in the parish, and his eldest three sons were born there.

1. Mary, b. 23rd May, 1767, d. 7th February, 1768.
2. Janet, b. 4th December, 1771, d. 30th June, 1772.
3. Grace-Orangebay, b. 26th May, 1774, d. unmarried 24th March, 1849.
4. Margaret, b. 26th July, 1776, d. 4th October, 1861, having m. the Rev. Francis Stewart, Minister of Craignish, and had issue. —See below.

Duncan Campbell of Duchernan was succeeded by the eldest surviving son of his brother the Rev. Peter Campbell, viz.:

VIII. James Campbell, Lieut. R.N., b. 17th July, 1768, served heir 16th November, 1798 (see p. 38), who, dying unmarried 15th September, 1818, was succeeded by the elder son of his next brother, George, to whom we revert.

The Rev. George Campbell (see p. 37), Minister of Ardchattan and Muckairn, Argyllshire, 1796-1817, was b. 17th May, 1769, and d. at Long-Ashton, near Clifton, in Somersetshire, 31st January. 1817. By his wife, Jane. daughter of Duncan MacDiarmid, Esq. Glenure, representative of the MacDiarmids of Glenlochay, he had :

1. Peter-Colin, D.D., Principal of the University of Aberdeen, married 1838, Jessie, eldest daughter of the Hon. James Wylie, of Burnside-Ramsay, Canada, Member of the Legislative Council of that Colony, and has had issue :—
    1. George-MacIver, M.A., M.B., Assistant Surgeon, 85th King's Light Infantry Regiment, d. unmarried at Meean Meer, India, 6th December, 1863, aged 26, beloved and lamented by all who knew him.*
    2 and 3. James-Wylie and Peter-Colin, twins, d. in infancy.
    4. Donald-Daniel-MacIver, Bengal C.S. and of Lincoln's Inn, m. 1871, Effie-Julia, eldest daughter of the late George-William Branscombe, Esq., and has issue.
    5. William-Macdonald-MacIver, M.A.
    6. Colin-MacIver.
    1. Jane-Macdiarmid, m. 1860, Robert Smith, Esq , M.D.. son of the Rev. Robert Smith, D.D., Senior Minister of Old Machar, and has issue.
    2. Mary-Hamilton, m. 1867, Alex. Cochran, Esq. of Balfour, Co Aberdeen, and has issue.
    3. Margaret-Elizabeth-Graham. m. 1872, Granville Toup Nicolas, Commander R.N., son of the late Rear Admiral John Toup Nicolas, C.B., K.C.F. & M . &c. and has issue.
    4. Jessie Hamilton, d. young, 12th January, 1856.
    5. Grace-Alexina.
    6. Matilda-Augusta, d. in infancy.

* A memorial of their esteem and affection was erected over his grave by the Officers of the 85th Regiment. For an obituary notice, which appeared in the *British Medical Journal* of 6th February, 1869, see note at the end of this volume.

2. Duncan, M.D. of Edinburgh, residing at Toronto in Canada, Vice-President of the Medical Council of the Province of Ontario, married 1834, Matilda Winter, and has issue living :
  1. George-Andrew, M.D., Surgeon R.N., m. 1868, Mary Watson, third daughter of Charles Mactaggart, Esq., M.D. and has issue, a son, Donald-M'Calman, and two daughters.
  2. John-Macdiarmid, of the Inland Revenue Dept., Canada
  3. Lorne-Colin, M.D.
  4. Frank-Alexander.
  5. Arthur-Dalziell.
  1. Louisa-Grace.
  2. Augusta-Mary.
  3. Margaret-Eliza, m. 1871, Edmund-Alexander Campbell, Captain, Madras Army, second son of James A. Campbell, Esq. of New Inverawe, and has issue.
  4. Jessie-Matilda.
  5. Edith-Helen, m. 1870, Lieutenant-Colonel John Smith, Bengal Staff Corps, eldest son of the Rev. Robert Smith, D.D., senior Minister of Old Machar, and has issue.
  6. Gertrude-Rose.
3. George-James, an officer in the H. E. I. Co.'s Maritime Service, thereafter Merchant, Magistrate, and Vice-Consul for the U.S. at Puerto-Maria, Jamaica, where he died of sunstroke, June, 1841, unmarried and deeply regretted.
1. Margaret, married, 1838, the Rev. Peter Mackiehan, Minister of Lochgilphead, who died 1842, and has surviving issue a son, John, of Yulangah, Victoria, Australia, who m. 1868, Susan, dr. of David Hutton, Esq. of The Cheviots, Victoria, and has issue : 1, Margaret-Campbell ; 2, George-MacIver ; 3, David-Hutton.
2. Grace Jane, married, 1835, Alexander Campbell Stevens, Esq., who died without issue May, 1853.
3. Augusta-Murray, died young, 20th December, 1824.

On the death, in 1818, of James Campbell, Lieut. R.N., the representation devolved on his nephew :

IX. Peter-Colin Campbell, now D.D. Principal of the University of Aberdeen, served heir 1819.

Margaret, youngest daughter of the Rev. Peter Campbell, and sister of the Rev. George Campbell, m. the Rev. Francis Stewart, Minister of Craignish, and had one son and six daughters, viz. :
  1. Archibald-Francis Stewart, Minister of Aberfoyle, who m. Jane, second daughter of Robert Brown, Esq. of Whitsome-

L

Newton, Co. Berwick, and has issue one daughter, Elizabeth-Thomson, and five sons:

1, Francis-Archibald, Lieut. 1st W. I. Regt., who m. his cousin, Grace-Jane, daughter of George Malloch, Esq., and has issue, a son, Archibald-Francis, b. 1871. 2, Robert, in New Zealand. 3, Thomas-Brown, formerly Lieut. 30th Regiment, now Deputy Commissary, H. M. Control Dep., who m. 1872, Margaret-Milborough, daughter of Sigismund de Pass, Esq. of Kingston, Jamaica. 4, George-James, L.R.C.P. & S.E. Edin. 5, Hamilton, Student of Medicine.

1. Margaret, m. Dugald Sinclair, Esq. and had one daughter, Margaret, who died in infancy.
2. Elizabeth, m. George Malloch, Esq., Barrister, and Judge of the Leeds and Grenville County Courts, Canada, and has issue living:

    1, Francis-Stewart. 2, Archibald-Edward, M.D., Hamilton, Canada. 1, Grace-Jane, m. her cousin, Francis-Archibald Stewart (see above), and has issue.
    2, Elizabeth.
3. Grace.
4. Isabella-Macleod, m. the Rev. Duncan Campbell, Minister of North Knapdale, and has one son, John-Archibald, M.D., and five daughters: 1, Margaret. 2, Catharine, m. the Rev. James B. Mackenzie, Minister of Colonsay, now of Kenmore, and has issue one son, Duncan-Campbell. 3, Eugenia. 4, Jane-Macdiarmid. 5, Isabella-Emma.
5. Colina.
6. Janet-Mary.

Sub-Cadets of the MacIvers-Buey or Campbells of Quoycrook and Duchernan.

The MacIver Campbells of *Thurso, Lochend,* and *Castlehill,* in Caithness.*

I. Donald Campbell, styled "the Elder," Merchant in Thurso, is supposed to have been a son or grandson of John, the younger son of Kenneth Buey. He was certainly a near relative of the Quoycrook family, and his descendants and those of Patrick Buey correspond as "cousins" down to 1742. From the wide intervals between the dates of the baptisms of his children in the Thurso Register, he would appear to have been more than once married. He had the following issue baptized:

1. William, baptized 25th October, 1647. Witnesses—William Sinclair of Brimms, and John Innes of Blackhill—See below.
2. Elspeth, 19th October, 1660. Witnesses—Alexander R———, Chalmerlane to the Earl of Caithness, and John Murry.

* For much information as to this family, the writer is indebted to John Henderson, Esq., W.S., of Thurso, who has devoted great attention to the accurate investigation of the much-neglected family history of Caithness.

3. Ma . . 16th October, 1661. Witnesses—Mr. William Campbell (Minister of Olrick)* and Alexander Boynd.
4. Hugh, 18th November, 1662. Witnesses—Mr. Hugh Munro (Minister of Durness) and Mr. Neil Beaton (Minister of Dunnet). Hugh appears to have died young.
5. John, 10th April, 1672. Witnesses—John Sinclair of Ratter and and John Forbes of Torrisdaill. John became Commissary of Caithness (see p. 33), and purchased the estate of Castlehill, in the parish of Olrick, from the Earl of Breadalbane. He m. Anne, daughter of William Sinclair of Ratter,† and widow of Robert Sinclair of Durran. By her he had one son, Colin Campbell of Castlehill, who d. s. p. and two daughters, co-heiresses of their brother, 1, Isabel, who m. James Campbell of Balbreck (Barrock ?), 2, Janet, who m. James Budge of Toftingall, but had no issue.

II. William Campbell, eldest son of Donald, became Heritable Sheriff-Clerk of Caithness (see p. 33). He married, 1st, Elizabeth, daughter of James Murray of Pennyland, by whom he had a son, Donald, writer in Thurso, who d. s. p. after 22 April, 1704.‡ 2ndly, Helen Mowat, by whom he had six sons :

1. James, of Lochend, see below, baptized 6 Nov. 1685. Witnesses— James Campbell, Bailie of Thurso,‖ and . . . .
2. William, in the Admiralty, Secretary to Admiral Vernon. He had a son, Alexander, Captain R.N., whose only son, also named Alexander, succeeded to Lochend in 1776, on the death of his cousin, Oswald Campbell.
3. John, 21 May, 1688. Witnesses—John, Lord Glenorchy, and . . . Muschet. He died unmarried.
4. Patrick, b. . . 1689, was alive in 1705, when he witnesses a deed relative to Quoycrook, after the death of Patrick Buey. He appears to have died unmarried.
5. Colin, b. 29 May, 1691. Witness—Mr. John Campbell (of Castlehill) Commissary of Caithness (his uncle). Died unmarried.
6. Hugo, b. . . 169— was Joint Heritable Sheriff-Clerk with his brother, James, at the abolition of the Heritable Jurisdictions. He m. Jean, daughter of John Sinclair of Forss, and had two sons and two daughters : 1, John, served heir to his uncle James and his cousin, Oswald of Lochend, 26 February, 1777— apparently by mistake—his cousin, Alexander, son of Captain Alexander Campbell, R.N., being the real heir—see below. John

---

* A native probably of Moray or Nairn, not supposed to have been a relative.

† She was served, 20th June, 1713, heiress portioner special to her brother, David Sinclair of Freswick (who died, April, 1712) in the estates of Freswick and patronage of Canisbay; also, heiress general, 16th October, 1716.

‡ Donald's name is entered in the Register at the same time with his half-brother's, James, 6th November, 1685. Probably he had been baptized in private and the registration omitted.

‖ Supposed a Perthshire Campbell, not a relative.

appears to bave d. s. p.   2, Rose, Merchant in Spain. 3, Isabella,
died unmarried. 4, Elizabeth, m. Colonel Grant, but bad no issue.

III. James Campbell, eldest surviving son of William, succeeded his fatber as
Heritahle Sberiff-Clerk of Caithness. He acquired the estate of Lochend
in tbe parisb of Dunnet. He m. 1st, Mary, daughter of John Sinclair
of Forss (wbose sister was married to bis brother, Hugo), but by her had
no issue. 2ndly, Isabella, daugbter of the Rev. James Oswald, Minister
of Watten, sister of Richard and Alexander Oswald of Glasgow and of
Scotstown, county of Renfrew, and cousin-german of Ricbard Oswald of
Auchencruive, Commissioner Plenipotentiary for negociating the Peace of
Paris hetween Great Britain and the United States. By her he had two
sons, William and Oswald. He died in 1766, and was succeeded by his
elder son :

IV. William Campbell of Lochend, served beir to bis father 16 June, 1768.
Dying s. p., be was succeeded by his only brotber :

V. Oswald Campbell of Lochend, served beir 15 Marcb, 1770, d. s. p. in 1776,
and was succeeded by :

VI. Alexander Campbell of Lochend, only son of Captain Alexander C.,
R.N., only son of William, 2nd son of William, first Sheriff-Clerk of the
family. He was served beir to his cousin, Oswald, 26 September, 1777,
and in 1778 sold the estate to Sinclair of Freswick. At his death, the
male line of the older Tburso family is snpposed to bave become extinct.

Tbe MacIver Campbells of *Dorary, Brubster, Thurso (younger family), Biaal-
byne, Shurary, Braehour, Liurary,* connected with the Quoycrook family,
and of whom some are supposed to bave descended from William Buey.

Dorary. Between 1650 and 1680 tbe following beads of families, probably
brothers, are on record :

1. William Campbell, styled " William Beag," or " the Little." He removed before 1677 to Bruhster. He bad, besides a younger son,
Donald, baptized 18 July, 1664, two who attained manhood.

1. Murdoch, of Tofthorsa, who m. Anna, daughter of Patrick
Buey Campbell of Quoycrook, and had issue—see above.

2. Alexander, who appears to have remained at Brubster, to
whom Donald Campbell of Aimster, the Cbamberlain, ac-
knowledges a debt in 1704.

This family appears to bave been in wealtby circumstances.

2. Donald Campbell, wbo had the following cbildren baptized :

1670, 14 October, Farqubar. Witnesses—William Campbell,
Merchant in Tburso, and Donald Campbell, younger there—
see below.

1673, July, K . . .   } Witnesses—William Campbell, in
Tbe same day, James. } Tburso, and .   .   .   .
1676, 23 October, Katharine. Witnesses—William Campbell,

Notary in Thurso (afterwards Sheriff-Clerk), and William Campbell, Merchant in Thurso.

1677, 28 May, William. Witnesses—Murdo (afterwards of Tofthorsa) and Alexander Campbell in Dorary.

3. John Campbell, who had a dr., Agnes, baptized 14 October, 1670. Witnesses—William Campbell, Merchant in Thurso, and Donald Campbell in Dorary.

4. Neil Campbell in Dorary, who is a witness in 1672, was probably also a brother. He may be the same as Neil MacIver, to whose dr. Anne's marriage contract, in Oct. 1689, Patrick Campbell of Quoycrook is a cautioner.

Thurso, younger family, closely connected with the preceding :

1. William Campbell, Merchant in Thurso, who had a son, John, baptized 20 February, 1672 ; a daughter, Marie, 9 April, 1675 ; and a daughter. Barbara, 2 January, 1682. The last may be the same who married an Alexander Campbell, contract dated May 8, 1705.

2. Donald Campbell, the younger, Merchant in Thurso. Has a son, James, b. 24 Nov. 1663 ; Angus, b. 7 Dec. 1665, He is probably the same as the Donald Campbell in Scrabster, who, 3 March, 1671, has a child baptized—Bessie—the same as Donald Campbell, in Lynester,* who has a son, John, baptized 17 June, 1673— and the same also as Donald C. of Lybster, to whom his grand-nephew, Neil Campbell, son of William C. in Shurarie, is served heir male general, 17 July, 1732.

As William and Donald appear as witnesses at the baptism of children of the Dorary Campbells mentioned above, a near relationship may be presumed.

Braalbyne. Kenneth Campbell, who possessed Braalbyne, witnesses, 17 April, 1665, a sasine in favour of Patrick Campbell of Quoycrook, from which circumstance it is inferred that he was a relative. He may have been the father of John Kennethson in Halkirk, who witnesses along with him.

Shurary. 1711, 11 July, James Campbell in Shurary is cautioner in the marriage contract of a Farquhar M'Iver and Janet Campbell (probably daughter of James), in the parish of Reay. He was, it is thought, a near relative of William and Donald Campbell the younger, above mentioned. He died in 1738.†

* Evidently Lybster, near Thurso, at the mouth of the water of Forse

† Tombstones at Reay bear the following inscriptions:—" Here rests the dust of ane honest gentleman, William Campbell, who departed this life, . . November, 1670." " Here lyes the dust of James Campbell, sometime in Shurery, who departed this life, 16th of May, 1738." This stone bears the Argyll Arms, but with the quarterings transposed.

1732, July 17, Neil Campbell, son of William Campbell in Shurarie, is served heir male general to his grand uncle, Donald Campbell of Lybster, Merchant, Thurso.

The Iverachs or Campbells of *Braehour*, &c.

The family of the Clan-Iver in Caithness, which bears the name of Iverach, possessed the farm of Braehour, in Halkirk, from which it was designated, for two or three generations in the 17th century, and then removed to Clayock, in the same parish ; one member of the family living at Braalbyne, and another possessing Liurary. Tradition appears to connect an ancestor of this family with the foray of 1666 (see p. 30), thus suggesting a possibility of its descent from " John-Mac-William-Mac-Iver in Achness," a younger son of William Buey. * The representative, in the earlier half of last century, was William Iverach or Campbell, in Sordale, whose son, Peter Iverach (Auchingills)—born 1744, died 1841, æt. 97—married Barbara Waters, and had by her :

1. Donald Iverach or Campbell, who died 1816, leaving a son, Peter (Weydale), who is married and has issue.
2. William, who left issue.
3. John, born 1755, died in infancy.
4. John (Weydale), born 1776, died 1860, married 1799, Anne Manson, by whom he had (besides a dr. Barbara, who m. James Swanson, and had issue) :
   1. Peter, who died 1869, and left issue alive, a son, William, and a daughter, who both m. and have issue.
   2. James, who has five sons · 1, John, m. and has issue ; 2 David ; 3, James, M.A., Minister of the Free Church at West Calder, m. and has issue; 4, Peter ; 5, Donald ; and six daughters, the two eldest m. and have issue.
   3. Donald, died unmarried.
   4. John, died in infancy.
   5, William, of Wideford, born 1810, married 1835, Elizabeth, eldest daughter of John Guthrie of Wideford, Orkney, and has the following issue alive :
      1. John-Guthrie, married 1859, Mary-Hamilton, daughter of Dr. A. R. Duguid, by whom, who died 1867, he has surviving a son, William, and two daughters, Mary-Elizabeth and Margaret-Guthrie.†
      2. William, M.A., Edinburgh, Student of Divinity, died 1863.
      3. James, M.A., Edin., Student of Divinity, died 1870.
      1. Anne, married Dr. W. B. Robertson, and has three sons living, John, William, and James.
      2. Margaret-Guthrie.
      3. Elizabeth, died in infancy.

* At Trostan, " Here lies the body of Robert Iverach in Liurcry, 1676." " Here lies the body of Robert Iverach in Liurery, 1748."

† The author desires to record his great obligations to Mr. John Guthrie Iverach, for valuable assistance in his researches into the history of the Clan in Caithness.

From the MacIvers Buey also is supposed to have been descended William Campbell of Ausdale, who lived, in the last century, to the age of 84, and had, in his own time, 19 children, 98 grand-children, and 33 great-grand-children, as is stated by Robert Mackay in his " History of the House of Mackay" p. 560. One of his sons, Alexander, in Thurso, was the father of Barbara, wife of the aforesaid Robert Mackay, and of Sir William Campbell, who died Chief Justice of Upper Canada, above forty years ago.

There are some detached notices of MacIvers and Campbells of MacIver origin in Caithness, but the ruinous state of the records, and especially the destruction of the parochial register of Halkirk, by the act of an incendiary, render it impossible to arrange them genealogically

Several Campbells, of Perthshire and Moray origin, appear in Caithness in the 17th and 18th centuries. None of these are here mentioned, nor any who were not evidently MacIvers, and also presumably descendants of Kenneth Buey or his brother.

II. The MacIVERS BAYNE. Extinct. The genealogy is given fully on pages 38, 39.

III. The MacIVERS or CAMPBELLS of *Pennymore*—believed to be extinct. Iver MacIver of Pennymore witnesses, in 1513, a precept of Colin, and, in 1529, a Charter of Archibald, Earl of Argyll. His successors were: 1, John [?]; 2, Iver [?]; 3, John, who witnesses a wadset of Ardlarach in 1602; 4, Iver, who witnesses the same; 5, John, married Catherine, dr. of Thomas Robieson [Robertson?] of Saltcoats; 6, William, served heir Jan. 18, 1666, to Catherine Robieson his mother. He was succeeded by his sister, Jean, married, 1st, to Campbell of Clenary, who d. s. p.; 2nd, to the Rev. Patrick Campbell of Torblaren, Minister of Inveraray. and had issue: 1, Dugald, of Kilmory (see p. 36); 2, Duncan, Merchant in Glasgow; 3, Colin, of Knockbuy; 4, Colonel John, of Black-River; 1, Elizabeth, m. Colin Campbell, of Ederline; 2, Bessie, m. Colin Campbell, of Attichuan; 3, Jean, m. the Rev. Daniel Campbell, of Duchernan—see pp. 34-37. All had issue.

Clenary. Supposed to be a sub-cadet of Pennymore.—See p. 21. Besides the Major John Campbell there mentioned, there was another Major Campbell involved in the insurrection of 1685, who is said to have been of the Duntroon family. The Very Rev. Neil Campbell, only child of Major John Campbell, became representative (and apparently sole male survivor) of Pennymore after his uncle Clenary's death. He was brought up to the Church by the Rev. Patrick Campbell of Torblaren, Minister of Glenaray, above-mentioned, the husband of his uncle's widow. He was successively Minister of Kilmallie, Rosneath, and Renfrew, and was ultimately appointed, in 1727, Principal of Glasgow College, dying 22nd June, 1761, in the 59th year of his ministry. He m. Henrietta, 2nd daughter of Patrick Campbell of Kildusklan, by whom he had: 1, Patrick, bred to the Medical Profession, who d. s. p. in Jamaica; 2, Archibald, d. s. p.; 3, Colin, Minister of

Eaglesham, 1741-61, of Kilmaronock till 1769, of Renfrew from 1769 till 24th November, 1788, when he d., in the 71st year of his age and the 48th of his ministry, having m. 20th December, 1749, Elizabeth, daughter of the Rev. John Montgomerie, Minister of Stewarton, and had a son, John, and a daughter, Christian, of whom nothing further is known. 4, Duncan, who m. and had a daughter married to Colin Campbell, Merchant in Greenock (son of Alexander Campbell, 5th son of Sir James Campbell, Bart., of Auchinbreek), by whom she had three daughters, the eldest son of one of whom (Mrs. Stevens of Edinburgh), viz.: Alex. Campbell Stevens, m. Grace-Jane, daughter of the Rev. George Campbell, Minister of Ardchattan (see Quoyerook and Duebernan p. 83), and d. s. p. in 1853. Colin Campbell succeeded to the Auchinbreek Baronetcy on the death of the last Sir James in 1813 14, but, having no male issue, did not assume the title. 6, War-burton, and 7, John, both died young. 1st, daughter, Anne, m. John Somerville of Renfrew, and had issue. 2d, Mary, d. unmarried. The author has been unable to trace any male descendants of Clenary or Pennymore further down than John, the grandson of Principal Neil Campbell and son of the Rev. Colin Campbell.

IV. The MacIVERS or CAMPBELLS of *Ardlarach*—claim to have been in possession, as tenants and proprietors, for 500 years, from the 14th century. The genealogy from 1500 is as follows :

About 1500, 1, John ; followed by 2, John : 3, in 1581, Dugald Mac-Iain-Vic-Iain-Vic-Iver ; 4, John, who married a natural daughter of Ronald Campbell of Barchbeyan, and probably obtained Ardlarach in heritage as her dower ; 5, Iver, born 1607, d. 1689, æt. 82 ; 6, Iver-Og, born 1646, d. 1712, aged 76. He had two sons : 1, Neil. who married a daughter of Duncan Campbell of Asknish ; 2, Dugald, Minister of Kilmartin, 1690-1721. 7, Neil was succeeded by : 8, Angus ; 9, Dugald ; 10, Alexander, who had four sons: 1 and 2, Alexander and John, who d. s. p. in Jamaica ; 3, Dugald, who succeeded his brother, but d. unmarried ; 4, George, who succeeded Dugald, and d. 1851, leaving two sons, Dugald and George.

B. GLASSARY BRANCH OR BRANCHES.

I. The MacIVERS or CAMPBELLS of *Kirnan*.

Between 1500 and 1550, Alexander Mak Kyivir of Keyirnanae[h]—see p. 21 ; 2, 1581, John ; 3, 1616, Alexander ; 4, Archibald, " hæres Alexandri patris," in 1649, married Elizabeth, second daughter of the Rev. Dugald Campbell, Parson of Knapdale, by whom he had three sons ; 1, Alexander ; 2, Daniel, Minister of Kilmore, who married a daughter of Campbell of Ballygerran, and had one son and three daughters ; 3, John, Minister of Kilealmonell, who married Mary Liddell, but d. s. p.

Alexander Campbell of Kirnan, Commissary-Clerk of Argyll, married, 1st, Mary, eldest daughter of John Campbell of Kildalloig, who had no

issue except a daughter, Henrietta, married to Archibald Maclachlan of Kellenochanach ; 2nd, Margaret, daughter of Stuart of Ascog, in Bute, and widow of John MacArthur of Milton, by whom he had :

1. Robert, sometime in the Army, author of the " Life of John, Duke of Argyll and Greenwich," &c., died unmarried before 1750. He sold, in 1732, the four merklands of the two Kirnans, the merkland of Auchaleck and the twenty-shilling land of old extent of Kinlochlean to the Rev. Alexander Campbell, Minister of Glenaray, who d. May, 1734. The conveyance was executed only a considerable time afterwards in favour of the purchaser's son, Lieutenant, afterwards Captain, Duncan Campbell, served heir to his father, a second time, 24th August, 1745.

2. Archibald, D.D., Minister of the Scots Church, Jamaica ; removed, before 1772, to Virginia. He m. Elizabeth, daughter of William Mackay of Tuheg and Achoul, relict of Duncan Matheson of Shinness, and had, besides other children, George-Washington Campbell, who was District Attorney of the U.S., Secretary to the American Treasury, and Minister of the U.S. at the Court of St. Petersburg. The grandson of the Rev. Dr. Archibald, Frederick Campbell, succeeded early in this century, under an entail executed in 1763, to the estates of Whitcharony in Peeblesshire and Ascog in Bute, and had to take the additional name of Stuart.

3. Alexander, born 1710, died in Edinburgh, March, 1801, æt. 92 ; Merchant in Glasgow, m. 1756, Margaret (daughter of his partner, Daniel Campbell, of the Craignish family, born 1736, died 1812), and had eight sons and three daughters. The youngest son was Thomas Campbell, author of the " Pleasures of Hope," born 27th July, 1777, died at Boulogne, 15th June, 1844. See Beattie's "Life and Letters of Thomas Campbell."

II. The MacIVERS or CAMPBELLS of *Glasvar.*

1, Charles, h. c. 1472 ; 2, Archibald, h. c. 1507 ; 3, 1542, Alexander ; 4, 1592, John ; 5, Angus ; 6, John ; 7, Angus ; 8, 1691-93, John, (had two brothers, Charles and Alexander) ; 9, 1710-15, Angus, who had a younger brother, the Rev. Archibald, Minister of Kilmonivaig, 1720, of Lismore and Appin, 1724-52, when he died, aged about 60, having married Janet, eldest daughter of (Sir) Alexander Campbell (Bart.) of Airds and Ardnamurchan, but without issue ; 10, James, 1762-67. The direct line seems to have ended in an heiress, daughter of James. The Representative is unknown.

Sub-Cadets of Glasvar.

Letternamolt. Angus of Letternamolt, younger son of Alexander of Glasvar of 1542, and brother of the first John above-mentioned, married, 1592, Mariota, of the Craignish family.

Leckguary. Alexander Campbell of Leckguary is supposed to have been a brother of John of Glasvar (1691). He is mentioned in 1635, 1693,

M

and 1710. After this appears Malcolm C. of L, who has apparently a nephew, Alexander C., merchant in Glasgow. In 1776, another Alexander is served heir general to his grand-uncle, Malcolm C. of Leckguary. Charles Young, Merchant in Glasgow, acquired the property for a short time. At his death in 1787, it reverted to his nephew, Charles Campbell, the representative of the family and last Leckguary, also of Burnbank near Hamilton, Merchant in Glasgow, who married Flora, daughter of Duncan Campbell of Eskart afterwards at Cuilanlongart, by Isabel, youngest daughter of Angus Campbell of Asknish, and had issue four daughters :

1. Isabella-Ann, who inherited Leckguary, m. Neil Campbell, Major H.E.I.C.S., 4th son of Colin Campbell, Esq. of Kilmartin, and has had issue :
    1. Colin-Ward.
    2. Neil, m. and has issue.
    3. John-Alexander.
    1. Helen-Charlotte, md. 1st, Colin Campbell, Esq. of Kilmartin and Blackhall, and had issue, a son, Alexander Douglas, now of Kilmartin and Blackhall; 2nd, Douglas Wimberley, Esq., late of the 79th Highlanders, and has issue: 1, Colin-Campbell; 2, Charles-Neil-Campbell; 1. Marion-Gordon-Campbell; 2, Helen-Isobel-Campbell.
    2. Isabella-Janet.

2. Janet M'Kinnon, md. William Penney, Esq., afterwards Lord Kinloch, and left surviving issue, viz. :
    1. Charles-Campbell, Merchant, Bombay, who md. Louisa Campbell White, and has issue.
    1. Florence-Charlotte, md. Colonel H. Fraser, R.E., C.B., and has issue.
    2. Elizabeth-Ann, md. Allan M'Dougall, Esq. of Ardencaple, and has issue.
    3. Flora-Ann, md. Thomas Login, Esq., and has issue.

3. Sarah-Charlotte, md. Patrick Stevenson, Esq., and has issue :
    1. Florence, md. Thomas Webb Ware, Esq., and has issue.
    2. Janet-Muirhead, md. Travers Adamson, Esq., and left issue.
    3. Charlotte, md. George Dickson, Esq., and has issue.

4. Flora, md. John Eckford, Esq., M.D., H.E.I.C S., and had issue :
    1. John, Major R.E.
    1. Flora, md. Archibald Neil Campbell, of the Craignish Family, Colonel 48th Regiment, and has issue.
    2. Elizabeth-Allison, md. James Spaight, Esq.

Sub-Cadets of Kinnan or Glasvar.

Lagg. 23rd May, 1523, Malcolm M'Iver of Lagg witnesses a charter of Colin, Earl of Argyll, to Dugald, bastard son of Archibald Campbell of Craignish.

Achadakerlich. About 1600, Campbell of "Auchterharley" married the only daughter of David Graham of Grahamstown, 2nd son of Walter Graham of Gartur, 2nd son of Alexander, 2nd Earl of Menteith of the name. 1693-1710, Iver Campbell of A ; Alexander C., his brother.

Barmolloch. 1704, "Alexander Campbell, brother to Barmolloch" ; 1710-15. Malcolm Campbell of B. ; 1754, the Rev. Charles C. of Barmolloch, Minister of Tiree, married 13th June, 1757, Elizabeth Campbell. His only son, Robert, married Geillis, daughter of Campbell of Kilmartin, and had an only daughter, who m. ——— M'Lean.

Stroneskar. In 1657, Elspeth Campbell is served heiress to her father, Donald Campbell of Stroneskar ; 1704, Charles Campbell. Tutor of Stroneskar ; 1710, Colin Campbell of S. ; 1715, Charles C. of S.

Ulster. See at end of Cowal Branch.

ℭ. ꞘOWAL ꞖRANCH.

The MacIVERS or CAMPBELLS of *Ballochyle,* sometimes styled of *Strath-auchie,* * and *Dergachie,* near Dunoon, and of *Killride,* near Inveraray.

The first traceable of this family, Iver or Iwar M'Iver of Strathauchie, about 1481, appears to have had two sons :

1. John M'Iver of Dergachie, whose son, Iver (" Ewr Campbell M'Ean Vic-Ewre of Dergachie") acquired Ballochyle and Stronsaul in 1542,[†] and was alive in 1559, but seems to have d. s. p. and to have been succeeded by his cousin, Iver M'Alister Vic-Iver, 2nd son of his uncle, Alexander of Kilbride.

2. Alexander of Kilbride (near Inveraray), who had two sons : 1, Archibald or Gillespic-M'Alister-Vic-Iver, witness in 1538 to a charter of the Earl of Argyll to Ninian Bannatyne of Kaimes, succeeded to Kilbride and got a new charter from the Superior, Colin Campbell of Glenorchy, 16 May, 1561. His son. John M'Gillespic Vic-Alister-Vic-Iver, in 1572, resigns Kilbride in favour of his cousin Charles M'Iver-Vic-Alister-Vic Iver, and failing him and his issue to Charles's brother, Alexander. John appears to have d. s. p. 2. Iver M'Alister-Vic-Iver, who obtained Ballochyle after his cousin Iver-M'Iain-Vic Iver, and got a new charter from the Earl of Argyll in 1563.[‡] He had two sons : 1, Charles ; 2, Alexander.

Charles M'Iver of Ballochyle and Kilbride, elder son of Iver M'Alister, became the head of the branch on the death of his cousin, John

---

* Strath-Eachaig. † Orig. Par. ii. 67, 69.

‡ In 1559, "Archibald. Earl of Argyll, directs Vyr M'Cuir (sic) his Officiar of Strath-achie to pay to the Blak Freris of Glasgow twenty shillings for their annual rent of 1558." Orig. Par. II., 67.

M'Gillespic. He seems to have had two sons: 1, Alexander; 2, Robert, progenitor of the M'Ivers or M'Ures of Glasgow.

Alexander M'Iver succeeded his father in Kilbride and Ballochyle, and was served heir to an annual rent of £24 from Strondoran in Glendaruel, all in 1599. He had by his wife, Anna Campbell, (besides Archibald M'Iver or Campbell, heir apparent in 1639, who seems to have d. s. p. v. p.). two sons, Iver and Charles.

Iver (M'Alister) M'Iver of Kilbride and Ballochyle, resigns Ballochyle and Dallinlongart in 1658 to his brother, Charles.

N.B.—From this point the order of succession was given to the author by the late Colonel William Rose Campbell of Ballochyle :

I. Charles M'Iver or Campbell of Ballochyle, who m. Isobel Wallace, and had a son and successor :

II. Iver Campbell of Ballochyle, who is mentioned in the "Depredations on the Clan-Campbell" as having been plundered by the Jacobite invaders of Argyll under the Marquis of Athol in 1685-86. He had two sons, Charles and Alexander. He was succeeded, 24 Oct. 1718, by the elder, Charles.

III. Charles Campbell, called "Chearlaich-an-òir," or "Charles of the Gold," from his being supposed to have discovered a treasure. He sold Kilbride to John, Earl of Breadalbane. the Superior, for £990 Scots, in 1702. He was succeeded in 1744 by his son :

IV. Alexander Campbell, born and baptized 11 April, 1711. He was married in 1728, when only 17 years of age, to Violet, daughter of Duncan Campbell of Dergachie (Ardkinglas Branch), born 28 April, 1711, died aged 93 in 1803. They had five sons and ten daughters :

1. Daniel, who was disinherited by his father, and is said to have died in America.
2. Charles, Lieut. R.M., drowned on duty by the upsetting of a boat in Lamlash Bay, 4 Sept. 1760, aged 20.
3. Alexander, who succeeded.
4. Duncan ; 5, Lachlan, both died unmarried.

Of the daughters, the only one of whom there are descendants was Grisall or Grace, who m. John Graham (of the Duchray family) Captain in the 71st Highland Light Infantry, and had a daughter, Susan, m. to George Eddington, Captain 1st Royal Scots. Their son, John Eddington, also Captain in the Royal Scots, now of Ballengeich, Framlingham, Victoria, Australia, m. 1st, Mary-Elizabeth, daughter of Captain Smollett Campbell, 42nd Regiment, a younger son of Campbell of Craignish. She died in giving birth to a son, who died very young. Captain Eddington m. 2nd, Ann, daughter of James Blair, Esq., who

died in 1849 at Ballengeich, leaving three sons and one daughter, viz :

1, George-M'Lachlan Eddington, died unmarried, 4 June, 1853; 2, Archibald-Campbell Eddington; 3, Harry-Graham Eddington, m. Ann-Eliza Braim, daughter of the Ven. Archdeacon Braim, and has issue ; 1, Violette-Elizabeth.

Captain John Eddington, who, when very young, carried the colours of the 1st Royal Scots at the battles of Nagpore and Maheidpore, and saw much hard service in India, emigrated to Australia in 1839. His sister, Miss Susan Eddington, is also in that Colony.

Alexander Campbell of Ballochyle, d. in 1795, and was succeeded by his third son :

V. Alexander (2nd), D. L. for Argyllshire, b. 16 May, 1749. He m. Mary Campbell, daughter of Archibald Campbell, of the Ardintenny family, (who d. 13 April, 1811), and had :

1. Alexander, b. 14th Oct., 1777, who succeeded.
2. Archibald, b. 26 March, 1772, Captain 1st Royal Scots, d. unm. at Berbice 7 Feb. 1795.
3. Robert, b. 24 August 1782, Lieutenant 1st Royal Scots, d. unm. at St. Helena 2 September, 1809, on his return from India.
4. Charles, b. 3 May, 1784, d. in infancy.
1. Susan, b. 26 May, 1776, m. 1803, John Colquhoun, M.D. of Torrs, Physician in Greenock, and d. s. p. 2 Nov. 1836.
2. Violet, d. young.
3. Mary, d. unmarried at Greenock, 30 March, 1840.

Alexander (2nd), a man of great wit and humour, was Lieutenant-Colonel of the Argyll Volunteers. He d. 30 June, 1811, and was succeeded by his son :

VI. Alexander (3rd), Lieutenant-Colonel of the Argyllshire Militia, but retired in 1811. He m. Elizabeth-Forbes Rose, 11th daughter of William Rose, Esq., Representative of the Roses of Ballivet, (she m. 2ndly, Major William Murray), and had :

1. Alexander, b. 30 July, 1812, who succeeded.
2. William-Rose, b. 7 Sept. 1819, of whom below.
3. Mary, m. Henry Vibart, Esq., Madras C. S., and has issue :
    1, Alexander-John, Capt. Bombay Staff Corps ; 2, Henry-Meredith, Capt. R. E. (Madras.) 1, Juliana-Williams, m. Arthur Battye, Major Bombay Staff Corps, and has issue ; 2, Henrietta Campbell, m. Henry-Prowse Probyn. Lieut Bombay N. I., who d. s. p.
4. Violette, m. Lieut. (now Major-General) George Burn, of the Madras Army, and had :
    1, George-Campbell, d. young ; 2, Robert-Campbell, Capt. Madras Staff Corps, d. at Bankok ; 3 and 4, William-

Henry and Alexander-Rose-Tinné, d. young; 5, Frederick
Nicolls, Merchant in Burmab; 6, Walter-Hamilton;
and one dr., Violette-Anna, who m. Henry-Fane Sewell,
Capt. Madras Staff Corps, and has issue.

Alexander (3rd) d. 6 December, 1819, aged 42, and was succeeded by his
elder son:

VII. Alexander (4th), Ensign in the 55th Regiment, d. unmarried at Bellary,
8 February, 1833, and was succeeded by his only brother:

VIII. William-Rose Campbell of Ballochyle, Colonel in the Madras Staff
Corps, D. L. for Argyllshire, 1863, m. 1st, the Honourable Clementina-
Maria Arbuthnott, youngest dr. of John, 8th Viscount Arbuthnott, who
d. at Bolarum 23 Oct. 1851. having had one dr. Clementina-Rose, who d.
in infancy. He m. 2nd, Jane Morison, only child of the Rev. James
Buchanan, D.D., LL.D., and of Mary Morison, eldest dr. and beiress
of John Morison, Esq. of Hetland, Dumfries shire, and had:

1. Allister-Morison, b. 16, d. 21 September, 1863.
2. MacIver-Forbes-Morison, b. 1 June, 1867.
1. Mary-Morison.

With deep regret the author has to record the death of Colonel Campbell,
after a few days illness, at Edinburgh, 22 March, 1872, when the
representation of the family devolved on his only surviving son, Mac-
Iver-Forbes-Morison Campbell, now of Ballochyle.

Sub-Cadets of Ballochyle.

The McURES or MacIVERS of *Glasgow.*

Robert McUre, the first of this family, b. 1589, d. 17 March, 1634, æt. 96,
was "son lawful to Charles McUre, 'alias Campbel of Ballochyle, and
Janet Campbel." He m. Sarah Boyd of the family of Portincross in
Ayrshire, who d. 3 October, 1663. They had two sons: Thomas, said
to have been b. 1616, and Neil, baptized 8 April, 1626, who seems to
have died unmarried. Thomas m. Janet McEwan, daughter of John
McEwan, son of Baron McEwan of the family of Glenboig in Stirling-
shire, by Margaret Morrison, one of the numerous descendants attri-
buted by McUre to [the Honourable] Archibald Lyon of Glasgow, and
had three sons: 1, Robert, who d. s. p. aged 24; 2, John McUre,
Author of the "View of the City of Glasgow"; 3, Thomas, a painter
of promise, who was murdered in London in 1691, æt. 32.

John McUre, the Author, Keeper of the Register of Sasines, Glasgow, was b.
1656. He m. 1st, Janet, only daughter of Duncan Fisher (of Durren ?)
Chamberlain of Argyll, by whom he had three sons, of whom Robert,
the eldest and only one who appears to have reached manhood, m.
Marion, daughter of Sir John Campbell of Carrick, and died 2 August,
1708, aged 29, leaving three children, Robert, Thomas, and Helen,
who all died infants in 1709. John, the Author, m. 2ndly, Christian,

dr. of James Dunlop of Housebill, by his wife, Christian Hamilton, sister of Sir William H. of Whitelaw, Lord Justice Clerk. She d. s p. 26 December, 1730, æt. 65. He m. 3rdly, when above 73, Mary Stirling, eldest daughter of Mungo Stirling of Craigbarnet, by Marjory, daughter of Sir George Stirling of Glorat, Bart. She had no issue, and probably survived her husband, who d. May, 1747, aged 96, when the family became extinct. *

A pedigree of the Stirlings of Drumpellier says that John Stirling, Merchant in Glasgow (eldest son of John, and heir of his grandfather, Walter), born in 1640, m. 1663, Janet. dr. of Charles Campbell and his wife Elizabeth Hall, "which Charles was a son of the ancient family of Ballochoyl, Argyllshire, and a Captain under Charles II. at the battle of Worcester, where he was slain." The author of these pages has found no mention elsewhere of this Charles, and finds it difficult to assign him a place as *a son* of any representative of the family. It is barely possible that he may have been a son of the Charles who m. Isobel Wallace, and a younger brother of Iver who was plundered in 1635-86.

𝕭. or 𝕮. The MacIVERS or MacIVORS of *Glasslough* in Ulster.

Although the McIvers or McKeevers of Ireland generally—see pages 9 & 45— are a totally separate race from the Clan-Iver of Scotland, tracing their descent to a different Scandinavian progenitor of the same name, there appears no room to doubt that the family before us is of Scottish origin, and that its progenitor. a member of either the Glassary or Cowal division of the Clan, more probably the former, went from Argyllshire to Ireland soon after the plantation of Ulster, and settled at Glasslough in the County Monaghan.

His descendant (probably grandson) William McIver, is said to have seriously impaired the position attained by his predecessors.

James, the son of William, after spending some years in military service, early in last century, returned to Glasslough, and died there, having recovered a portion of the estate. He left a son—

John McIver, whose son—

James McIver, settled in Derry, where, as well as in Celeraine, he acquired considerable property. He left (with three daughters) three sons :

 1. John McIver, Lieutenant 61st Regiment, distinguished himself at the battle of Talavera, where he was severely wounded, and died in consequence. leaving, although married, no issue.

 2. William, died unmarried.

---

* These particulars have been extracted with some difficulty from the pages of McUre's Work, which is extremely confused and inaccurate in genealogical matters.

3. James, a man of great ability and culture, who left three sons and
    four daughters. Of the sons, two, John and Thomas, d. unmd.;
    the survivor and present representative of the family is—

The Rev. James McIvor, D.D., Rector of Ardstraw, Co. Tyrone, who, after
    a brilliant career as a Scholar of Trinity College, became Fellow in
    1844, and is now Professor of Moral Philosophy in the University of
    Dublin. Dr. McIvor is Author of "Religious Progress—Its Criterion,
    Instruments, and Laws (London, 1871)," and of various Tracts on
    Educational and other subjects. He married Pleasant, daughter of
    Charles Stewart, Esq. of Tullamore, a descendant of Colonel Stewart
    of the Siege of Derry, and has issue:

1. James, A. B., S. T. C. D., Barrister at Law.
2. Charles-Vernon, A. B , C. E., in the D. P. W., India.
3. Ivar, A.B., C.E., Sub.-Lieut. 3rd Hussars.
4. Stewart.

D. ROSS AND LEWIS BRANCH.*

I. The McIVERS of *Gress*, formerly of *Tournack* and *Leckmelm—Clann-a-
Mhaighstir.*

The family of Leekmelm, in the parish of Loch Broom, appears to have
always been regarded as the head of the numerous and important branch
of the Clan-Iver in Ross and Lewis.

1582, Jan. 24.—Evir M'Evir is presented by King James VI. to the
Vicarage of Fodderty†. He was the incumbent in 1601; how long thereafter is unknown. He is supposed to be the "Maighstear" from whom this
family are descended, and to have been proprietor of Leckmelm.

‡ 1635, Nov. 27.—Iver M'Iver of Culkenzie is served heir to his father,
"Iver M'Iver of Leckmalme."† This is probably "Imhear Mac-a-Mhaighstir," and the same as "Iver M'Iver in Lochbroom," who married a daughter

---

* The genealogical information given regarding the MacIvers of Lewis, has been
obtained mainly from Evander M'Iver, Esq. Scourie House; the late Rev. John M'Iver,
Kilmuir; Norman M'Iver, Esq., Stornoway; Miss Jane M'Iver, Stornoway, daughter
of the late Kenneth M'Iver of Tolsta; Mrs M'Donald, Bayhead; and the Rev. John
M'Rae, Minister of Stornoway; to all of whom the writer desires to acknowledge his
obligations.

* An anecdote omitted in the Notes, shewing the tenacity with which the M'Ivers
of Ross and Lewis retained their traditional attachment to Argyllshire, and their
singularly exalted idea of Kilmiebael-Glassary—the ancient *capital* of the Clan in
Argyll, now scarcely a village—may here be introduced. A humble member of the
race, arriving on the mainland, and being asked whence he came, is said to have
answered: "*Thainig mi o Stornua ann an Liughais, an baile 's mò 's an t'saoghal, ach
Cilemhichael mhòr Ghlasraith.*" " I have come from Stornoway in Lewis, the greatest
city in the world, except great Kilmichael in Glassary."

† Origines Paroch. ii., 470, 480

‡ Apparently a little before this time there is a "John M'Iver in Lochbroom," who
is the third husband of a daughter of Heetor Mackenzie, first of Meikleallan, and
whose daughter marries, about 1650, "Rorie MacIain-Vie-Alastair." See Appleeross
Genealogy of the Mackenzies.

of Roderick Mackenzie, second of Davochmaluag.* To him, or a son of his, tradition appears to trace the family of Tournack and Gress.

1663, Dec. 22.—" Murdoch M'Keiver of Lechmelme" is served heir to Donald M'Keiver his father. Soon after this, " Murdo M'Iver in Leckmelm," marries a daughter of Mr. John Mackenzie, Archdeacon of Ross.*

Evander M'Iver of Leckmelm, the last on record of the direct line, settled in Thurso about 1680. He had two sons, Murdo and John, and three daughters, Margaret, Janet, and Katharine, whose names are found in the baptismal register of Thurso. The sons appear to have died young ; of the daughters, Margaret married in 1705 Robert Key, a burgess of Elgin. Evander M'Iver of Leckmelm is witness to a bond at Thurso, 26 September, 1701. After this he cannot be traced, unless he be the person referred to in the note below.† From this time the representation of the branch has been regarded as belonging to the M'Ivers of Tournack or Gress (descended from Iver Mac-a-Mhaighstir), to whom we therefore turn. The names of the earlier heads of the family, who seem to have lived sometimes on their property of Tournack on Loch-Ewe, and sometimes at Gress, as hereditary tenants of the Seaforth family, have perished, but in the year—

1667.—" Evander Campbell, Insulan. Lewen." is admitted a student of the University and King's College of Aberdeen. There can be no doubt that this was the Iver M'Iver who was the head of the Tournack and Gress family, and who was born about 1650. The record is curious, as shewing that the theory of Campbell descent had by this time found its way as far as Lewis, although the name was not permanently adopted ‡

1680.—About this date, a daughter of Sir Kenneth Mackenzie of Coul, the first Baronet, is married to M'Iver of Tournack, doubtless the Evander above mentioned, and another daughter to Tournack's brother. Iver or Evander had two sons :

1. William, of Tournack, whose only son, Colin, was served heir male general to his father, William " of Tournaig," 6 Feb. 1769, but d. s. p.

2. John, of Gress, who became possessor of Tournack and representative on the death' s. p. of his nephew, Colin. He married Annabella, daughter of Charles Mackenzie of Letterewe, by Miss Cuthbert of Castlehill, and had :

   1. William, who married, first, a daughter of Mackenzie of Kildun, and had issue a son, Evander, who died unmarried.‖ By

---

* Genealogy of the Mackenzies, by the Laird of Applecross.

† In 1700, Evander M'Iver, "tacksman of the Scots Manufactory Paper Mills." presents to the Privy Council, along with James Watson, a petition for leave to reprint an English book entitled " A War between the British Kingdoms considered.' Chambers' Domestic Annals of Scotland, p. 215.

‡ Fasti Aberdonenses, 486.

‖ The celebrated Gaelic Poet, Robert Mackay (Rob Donn), alludes to his hospitable reception in Lewis by Mr. and Mrs. M'Iver, after an escape from perishing at sea in the Minch, in lines which show that the M'Ivers of Gress were then regarded as the heads of the Ross and Lewis Branch :

'Nuair ràinig sinne an t'àit,
Bha cuideachd pairteach ruinn,
Armunn ùr Chlann Imhcair,
'S nighean Triath Chill-Duinn.

The author is indebted to Mr. Archibald M'Niven, Schoolmaster, Scorraig. Lochbroom, for indicating this passage to him.

his second marriage, to a daughter of Mackenzie of Lochend, Poolewe, he had—1, John, who settled at Alexandria in Virginia, where he married and had a daughter, married to Major ———— Graham; 2, Annabella, commonly known as "Miss Annabella Tournack;" 3, a daughter, who married and had a daughter, Mrs. Corrigil, in Liverpool.

2. Evander (Iver) of Gress, who married Lillias, daughter of Mackenzie of Lochend, Poolewe, and had several sons, of whom Lewis alone left issue. He had also a daughter, Anne, married to Colin M'Iver (last) of Coll. See below, under Coll.

Lewis M'Iver succeeded his cousin John as representative of the family, and his father Evander as possessor of Gress. He married Catharine, daughter of James Robertson, Collector of Customs at Stornoway, son of the Rev. James Robertson, Minister of Lochbroom—celebrated for his loyalty, benevolence, and great bodily strength*—by whom he had (besides a dr. Lillias, who m. Roderick M'Leod, merchant in Liverpool, and has a dr. Annabella) seven sons:

1. Evander.
2. James, who married, and died leaving an only daughter, Lillias-Ann.
3. John, Secretary to the Madras Bank, who has two sons—1, Lewis, in the C. S. of Madras; 2, Iver-Ian.
4. Lewis, resident in Glasgow.
5. Murdo-Robertson, died unmarried.
6. Alexander, in Hong-Kong, m. 4 August, 1870, Marjory-Alexandrina Gunn, only daughter of the late Captain William Gunn, 93d Highlanders, and has issue: 1, William-Evander, 2, Catherine-Lillias.
7. William, died unmarried in China, 1849.

Lewis M'Iver died in 1845, aged 63, deeply regretted, and was succeeded in the representation of this family by his eldest son:

Evander M'Iver, Esq., resident at Scourie House, Deputy Lieutenant Co. Sutherland, who married Mary, daughter of Donald Macdonald of Skeahost, and has had issue:

1. James Robertson, Bengal Med. Serv. d. unm. at Sealkote, 11 Dec. 1869.
2. Donald, a youth of great promise, d. unm. 1865, æt. 23.
3. Duncan-Davidson.
4. Lewis, in the Madras Bank, Colombo.
5. Evander, d. unmarried 1868.
6. Murdo-Robertson, at the C. of Good Hope.
7. John-Macdonald.
1. Mary, m. 11 July, 1871, Francis Shand Robertson, Esq. of Dalkeith House, Richmond, Surrey, and has a dr. Mary-Catherine.

There are probably M'Ivers in Lewis, including some of those in the parish of Uig, who are offshoots of this stock, after its settlement in Lewis, although the connection cannot be traced.

---

* See New Statistical Account of Scotland. Art. Lochbroom.

There are also at Scorraig, in Lochbroom, in Ross-shire, a few M'Ivers who claim to be descended from this family. According to William M'Iver at Scorraig, who d. aged 89, 21 April, 1869, Leckmelm—having, as is alleged, ceased to belong to the original M'Iver proprietors—was acquired by a Captain Donald Roy M'Iver, whose son, Murdoch, made a fortune abroad, but was, through the loss of a ship in which his wealth was embarked, unable to retain his father's purchase. Murdoch's son, Donald, who lived in Contin, had two sons—1, Kenneth, whose only son, Donald, was the father of William the informant ; 2, John, who was a tenant on Tournack, when John M'Iver of Gress, great-grandfather of Evander M'Iver, Esq., the present representative of the Gress family, was possessor. John had two sons, Roderick and Kenneth, who both had issue, of whom the former settled in Sutherland, the latter in America. William M'Iver has left issue four sons. It is quite impossible to reconcile the details of this history with documentary evidence extant. Yet there seems reason, in the traditional feelings of the country, to believe that this family are, in some way, remotely descended from the Leckmelm family. Donald Roy, and his son Murdoch, the same doubtless as are mentioned above, under the date 1663, Dec. 22, were clearly the heirs male of the previous possessors of Leckmelm, not a new race, and Donald in Contin, if a son of Murdoch, can hardly have been legitimate.

II. The McIVERS of *Ness* or *Tolsta, Stornoway* or *Coll—Clann-a-Bhaillidh.*

Duncan McIver, the son of Kenneth, the son of John (Donncha Mac-Chainneaich-Vic-Iain) of Tolsta, the progenitor of this Branch, is said to have been a Judge or Sheriff at Ness, in succession to the ancient Breves, Baillies or Judges of Lewis. He had five sons—Alexander, Donald, Kenneth, William, and Roderick, who probably all left issue, but the descendants only of Alexander and Roderick have been found distinctly traceable. *Kenneth*

A. *Issue of Alexander, elder son of Duncan of Ness and Tolsta.*

Alexander McIver of Tolsta, said also to have been Sheriff of Lewis, was twice married, first very early, and again very late in life ; some of his grandsons by the first marriage being much older than his sons by the second. He had by his two marriages twelve sons, of whom several are said to have been Clergymen of the Church of Scotland. Through the destruction of the Ecclesiastical Records of the Outer Hebrides, no information regarding these has been obtained, although to their labours is no doubt to be ascribed the tradition of the MacIvers having been very instrumental in propagating the Protestant religion throughout Lewis. The sons whose names have been preserved, are : 1, Alexander, Baillie of Stornoway ; 2, Roderick, who succeeded as Sheriff at Ness ; 3, Donald, of Tolsta ; 4, John, Merchant in Stornoway ; 5, Murdo, and 6, William, both probably Clergymen. The only sons whose issue has been traced are Alexander, Donald, and John ; but there are probably many descendants of other sons.

a. Alexander McIver, Baillie of Stornoway, had one son :

John McIver, Baillie of Stornoway, who married Mary, daughter of Mackenzie of Kildun, and had four sons : 1, Alexander, Baillie of Storno-

way: 2, Colin, Minister of Glenelg; 3, Roderick, died unmarried; 4, George, drowned, unmarried. John was succeeded by his eldest son:

Alexander McIver, Baillie of Stornoway, and Major of the Lewis Militia. He married Margaret Downie, but dying without male issue, was succeeded in the representation of the family by his brother:

The Rev. Colin McIver, Minister of Glenelg, 1782-1829; J.P. for Inverness-shire, 1804; who married, 2 January, 1785, Anne, daughter of Donald M'Leod of Drynoch, and had issue:

*1. John (1), Captain 98th Regiment, died at Chichester, 1824, unmd.
2. Donald, sometime Lieutenant 70th Regiment, died 1844, married and left issue, all dead.
3. Norman, Lieutenant 8th W. I. Regiment, died 1837, unmarried.
4. George, Captain 42nd Regiment, died unmarried 1847.
5. Alexander, Minister of Dornoch, who succeeded his brothers, Donald and George, as head of the family, and died 1582, married Alexandrina Campbell, by whom he had a son, Kenneth, and a daughter, Anne, who married the Rev. Thomas Stephen, Minister of Kinloss, and has issue.
6. Colin, Planter at Benares, died unmarried 1837.
7. John (2), Minister of Kilmuir, in Skye, married 1st October, 1840, Jane Finlayson, youngest daughter of Dr. Alexander Macleod, Ballone, North Uist, and died 1870, having had issue:

1. Colin-John, b. 1843, d. 1853.	1. Anne-Mary, m. 1871, to the Rev. Allan R. Andrew, Rector of Milne's Institution, Fochabers.
2. Alexander, in India.	
3. Somerled.	
4. Fergus.	
5. Ewen.	2. Mary, b. 1844, d. 1855.
6. Donald, b. 1861, d. 1863.	3. Margaret.
	4. Jessie.
	5. Alexandrina.
	6. Anne-Jean.

The Rev. Colin McIver had also the following daughters:
1. Jessie, died unmarried, æt. 79.
2. Margaret, died unmarried, æt. 81.
3. Mary, married Ewen Cameron, Talisker, brother of the late D. C. Cameron, Esq. of Barcaldine, and has issue D. C. Cameron, Tacksman of Talisker and Kinlochnevis, in Knoydart.
4. Catharine, married Farquhar Robertson of Scalasaig in Glenelg (in Canada since 1823), and has issue. Three of their sons are in Australia.
5. Alexandrina, married Lauchlan Chisholm, late of Lochans in Moydart, now in Queensland, and has issue several sons and daughters.

* The eldest and youngest sons of the Rev. Colin McIver were both named John. His sons are said to have been all singularly handsome men more especially Captain George McIver of the 42nd Highlanders, and also, with the exception of the Rev. Alex. MacIver of Dornoch, to have borne a striking resemblance to each other.

The representative of this family, and the head of all the numerous descendants of Duncan MacKenneth·Vic-Iain, of Ness and Tolsta, is Kenneth M'Iver, Esq., now of Bombay, only son of the late Rev. Alexander M'Iver of Dornoch.*

b. Donald M'Iver of Tolsta, son of Alexander, son of Duncan of Ness. His sons were—1, Alexander, who died in the United States; 2, Kenneth, d. s. p· 3, John, Merchant in New York; 4, Evander, drowned near Stornoway, leaving a daughter, Evandrina; 5, Murdo, Minister of Lochalsh, 1770, married, 1st, 11 March, 1775, Mary, daughter of John Mackenzie of Hilton ; 2nd, Isabella, daughter of William Fraser of Boughton. The Rev. Murdo M'Iver was drowned in passing to Gruinard 12th Feb., 1790, aged 48, leaving a son, Donald, served heir to his father 25 July, 1792, a youth of great promise, who joined his uncle John, at New York, but died unmarried at Bermuda, and four daughters, of whom three were married, one of them being Mrs. M'Aulay, whose daughter is married to Norman M'Iver, Esq., Banker in Stornoway.

c. John M'Iver, son of Alexander, son of Duncan of Ness, came into possession of Tolsta after his brother Donald.   He was a man of singular probity and honour, and is said to have excelled all of his time in Lewis in personal strength.   He married a daughter of Mackenzie of Lochend, Poolewe, and had four sons—1, Donald, d. s. p. ; 2, Colin, d. s. p.; 3, Dr. Alexander, Stornoway ; 4, Lewis, d. s. p. ; also a daughter, Anne, married to Kenneth M'Iver, son of William of Coll—see below—who succeeded him in the possession of Tolsta.

Dr. Alexander M'Iver was a man of great public spirit and benevolence, and devoted his professional services to his native island for fifty years without fee or reward, except the universal gratitude and respect of its inhabitants.   He married Mary M'Leod, and had two sons—

1. Daniel, now in Stornoway, who m. Emily, dr. of Capt. Neil M'Kinnon, of the 93rd Regt., and by her (who d. in 1872) has a son, Walter.

2. Norman, Banker in Stornoway, who married Barbara M'Aulay, grauddaughter of the Rev. Murdo M'Iver of Lochalsh, and has issue Alexander Colin, now in Madras, and six daughters, of whom the second, Catharine, married, 1867, Dr. William M'Rae, of the Madras Medical Service, son of the Rev. John M'Rae, Minister of Stornoway, and has issue, 1, John-Lewis; 2, Norman; and the third, Helen-Isabella, m. 1873, Donald MacIver Murray, Esq. of Darjeeling, in India.

Dr. Alexander M'Iver had also several daughters who married, and had issue.

* In his " Sketches of the Coasts and Islands," I. 186, Lord Teignmouth relates that at a funeral entertainment, at which he was present, near Stornoway, in 1827, the health of the Rev. Colin McIver of Glenelg, who presided on the occasion, was proposed as the Chief of the Lewis MacIvers. He was certainly the Chief of the Ness or Tolsta division of the Clan, the most numerous in Lewis, and to which probably all the McIvers then present belonged. But he is said himself to have admitted the priority of the Gress family in reference to the McIvers of Lewis and Ross as a whole, probably as more directly representing the old McIvers of Leckmelm.

B. *Issue of Kenneth, younger son of Duncan of Ness and Tolsta.*

The M'Ivers of Coll, in the parish of Stornoway, are descended from Kenneth, the second son who left issue of Duncan MacKenneth-Vic-Iain. Kenneth, called sometimes " *Maighstear Cainneach,*" who is said to have been a Physician, and to have earned distinction abroad, had two sons—1, William; 2, Kenneth, who left no issue.

William of Coll, elder son of Kenneth, married Annabella, daughter of Colin M'Kenzie, son of the Rev. Geo. M'Kenzie, Minister of Lochalsh, and had three sons—1, Kenneth, born 14 Sept., 1759, died 7 Feb. 1842. He became possessed of Tolsta after John, son of Alexander above-mentioned, whose daughter, Anne, he married 15 Dec., 1788, but resided principally at Stornoway; 2, Colin, born 1767, who succeeded to the possession of Coll; 3, John, died unmarried; and three daughters—Janet, Anne, and Jane, all married to gentlemen of the name of M'Kenzie.

Kenneth (Stornoway and Tolsta), eldest son of William of Coll, married, 15 December, 1788. Anne, daughter of John M'Iver of Stornoway and Tolsta, by whom he had the remarkable number of twenty living children, of whom the following sons attained manhood:

1. John, who died in Canada, leaving a son, Kenneth, now in Ballarat, Australia (who is married and has issue), also several daughters, Anne, Sophia, and Susan, who m. and have issue.
2. Daniel, at Karachi, in India, m. 1845, Sarah Meighan, and has five sons: 1, Charles, in command of the Police Force of Upper Scinde; 2, Daniel, in Calcutta; 3, Kenneth, in the Telegraph Department of India; 4, William; 5, John; and three daughters: 1, Mary-Anne; 2, Sarah; 3, Mabel.
3. Alexander, lost at sea, 1820, d. s. p.
4. William, at Kingston, in Canada, 5 May, died 1868, having m. Isabella Butterworth, and leaving two sons, John-Butterworth and Kenneth, and a daughter, Anne-Annabella.
5. Kenneth, at Agra, m. 1st, 1848, Mary-Anne-Catharine Blackburn, eldest daughter of Charles Stout, Esq., H. E. I. C. S., by whom he has two sons: 1, Kenneth-M'Kinlay; 2, Charles-William; and three daughters: 1, Eliza-Jane, m. Capt. Alexander Lindsay of the 1st Bengal Cavalry, who d. 1872, leaving a daughter Annie-Jane; 2, Annie-M'Leod; 3, Mary-Isabel. Mr. M'Iver m. 2nd, 1864, Caroline-Amelia Harris, dr. of Capt. William Harris of H. M. Indian Service, and widow of Mr. Walter Horst, I. P. S., and by her has: 1, Donald-Colin; 2, Norman-Alexander; and a daughter, Florence-Emily.

Of Mr. Kenneth M'Iver's daughters, Anne, Louisa, and Jane still live in Stornoway. To Miss Jane M'Iver, the writer is very greatly indebted for information. Four were married, viz.: 1, Margaret (Mrs. Murray), who had five sons, of whom there are three in India. and two daughters; 2, Mary (Mrs. Mackenzie), who had no issue; 3,

Janet (Mrs. M'Pherson), who had two sons and three daughters—the eldest m. to John-Kenneth M'Iver in India—see below; 4, Williamina (Mrs. Miller), who had five sons (of whom four are in Glasgow and one at sea) and two daughters, the elder of whom is m. to James Cassidy, Esq., Manager of the Bank of Upper India, Lucknow.

Colin (Coll), second son of William, married Anne, daughter of Evander 7th and sister of Lewis 8th of Gress. He emigrated to Canada in 1838, and died in 1859, aged 81, having had eight sons, of whom four survive.

1. William, formerly in India, now residing at Melbourne, Canada.
2. Evander, who died at Montreal, having m. Margaret, eldest daughter of the Rev. William Macrae, Minister of Barvas, and leaving 1, John-Kenneth, in India, who m. and has issue a son, Evander-John ; 2, Colin, in Toronto, Canada.
3. John, died young at Stornoway.
4. Kenneth, died in Australia unmarried.
5. Colin, near Melbourne, m. Jessie, eldest dr. of William Thomson, Esq. Hillend, Greenock, and had issue a son, who d. 1867, and a daughter.
6. Lewis, m. Sarah Pope, a native of Canada, and has issue one son and one daughter. He lives at Robinson, Canada.
7. John-Mackenzie, also at Robinson, Canada.
8. Alexander, died at Stornoway, having m Hannah Taylor, a native of Canada, and leaving issue a daughter.

Mr. Colin M'Iver had also two daughters, 1, Lily-Anne, resident at Melbourne ; 2, Annabella, deceased, who m. John Kingan, Esq. Montreal, and left issue one daughter.

The representative of the family of Kenneth, younger son of Duncan Mac-Kenneth Vic-Iain of Ness, is Kenneth M'Iver, Esq. Ballarat, Australia.

III. The McIVERS of *Uig.*

The members of the Clan who settled in the parish of Uig, and possessed, along with portions of the Mainland of Lewis there, some islands on its Western Coast, are said to have been partly of the Gress and partly of the Ness stock, but no exact genealogical distinction has been found possible. Of the families traceable to Uig, the most important are the MacIvers of Liverpool. Of these there are two families, related to each other, of which the one held at the end of the last and the beginning of the present century, and the latter now holds, a very high position in the business and maritime enterprise of the city. The author of these pages was informed by the late Rev. John M'Iver of Kilmuir in Skye, that one of the elder family and his father, the Rev. Colin M'Iver of Glenelg, traced a relationship to each other, and that the former was of the Ness stock.

A. The McIVERS of *Liverpool, Elder family.*

This family derives its origin from Iver M'Iver, believed to have been a native of Uig, who settled at Dunoon, early in the last century, and acquired a small property there. His son, John M'Iver, a merchant in Greenock, much respected for his integrity and benevolence, died at the age of 45, leaving three sons: 1, Iver; 2, Peter; 3, William.

Iver and Peter settled in Liverpool, and became prosperous merchants and shipowners, having at one time almost a monopoly of the trade between Liverpool and Glasgow. They were joined by their brother William, who after the death of both without issue, became the head of the house. He was a proprietor and freeholder, and patron of the Church and Parish of Kilmacolm, in the County of Renfrew, in the early part of this century. He married Anne Clark, by whom he had (besides a daughter married to the Rev. Jones Parry, of Madrin Park, Co. Carnarvon, and who d. Oct. 1872), an only son:

The Rev. William M'Iver, Rector of Lymm, Cheshire, 1845, who married Mary Stuart Smith, and died 1863, leaving issue:

1. Iver, late Captain 14th Regiment, d. 1868.
2. Stuart-William, Captain, Madras Army, married 1867, E. Agnes, daughter of J. Jennings, Esq. of Townhope, Co. Hereford, and has issue a son and a daughter.
3. William, in Liverpool, m. 19 April, 1870, Eleanor-Charlotte, third daughter of A. Thomson, Esq. of Liverpool.
4. Kenneth.
5. Colin.
6. John-Donald.
1. Flora-Zoé, married 1863, J. W. Fox, Esq of Girsby Manor, Co. Lincoln, and Statham Lodge, Cheshire, late Captain 12th Lancers. She d. without issue in Dec. 1868.
2. Margaret-Cunningham, married 1867, J. D. Dewhurst, Esq., second son of G. C. Dewhurst, Esq. of Beechwood, Lymm, Cheshire, and Aberuchill, Perthshire, and has issue a son and a daughter.
3. Annie-Graham.
4. Mary-Stuart, d. unmarried, 9 September, 1871.
5. Agnes.

B. The McIVERS of *Liverpool, Younger family.*

The progenitor of this family, now for five generations honourably connected with the maritime enterprise of the country, was Charles MacIver, apparently a nephew of Iver McIver of Dunoon above-mentioned. The son of a sea-captain, he was himself bred to the sea, and commanded a ship out of the Clyde. He had seven or eight sons, of whom only three grew up, who all followed him in the same profession. The eldest of these, John, earned a very high reputation by his skill and gallantry in command of the "Swallow," a ship of 14 guns, and other armed vessels, in the Government Service. He died without issue, as also did a younger

brother, who served for a time under him with the same credit, and afterwards commanded a ship.* The only son who left issue was:

David, who, like the other members of this family, was an intrepid and skilful mariner, and who perished in command of a ship in the Bay of Biscay in 1812. He married Jane, daughter of John Boyd of Port-Glasgow, who, when in command of a merchant ship, volunteered his services on board of a Man of War of the convoy on the occasion of an attack by a French squadron. The attack was successfully repelled, but Captain Boyd was killed in the action at an early age. David MacIver left, with three daughters, of whom Jane (who m. Robert Cowan, Esq.) and Margaret still survive, the following sons:

1. John, bred in the Office of the American Consul in Greenock; went to the United States when about 21, and died there unmarried about the age of 33, having acquired considerable property in land.

2. David, brought up in the same house as his brother John, removed to Liverpool when young, and founded, with the aid, after some years, of his younger brother Charles, the house now so well known in connection with Liverpool and Glasgow, and with transatlantic maritime enterprise. David, who like his brother, was beloved and respected by all who knew him, died unmarried at the age of 35.

3. Charles MacIver, now representative of the family and head of the house, m. Mary-Ann, youngest daughter of the late D. Morison, Esq. (of the Morisons of Lewis), Comptroller of H. M. Customs, Glasgow, and has issue:

   1. David, who married Annie, daughter of Robert Rankin, Esq.† of Liverpool, and by her (who died in 1869) has two sons. Charles and Robert-Rankin, and a dr. Helen.

   2. John, married Eliza-Mary, daughter of John Bulkeley Rutherford, Esq. of London. and has issue one dr.

   3. Charles.   4. Henry.
   5. William.   6 Edward.

   1. Jane, married William Ritchie, Esq. of Middleton, Co. Edinburgh.

   2 Marianne.   3. Elizabeth.

IV. Other MoIVERS of *Lewis* origin.

Among the Lewis members of the Clan must be noted:

1. The late Roderick McIver, Esq. Collector of Customs at Thurso, previously at Stornoway, two sons of whom settled in America; one,

* It is uncertain to which of the brothers the following paragraph in the Edinburgh Advertiser of 23 March, 1795, refers:—"The armed ship in His Majesty's Service, King Grey, commanded by the gallant Captain M'Iver, was sunk by a bombshell and part of her crew drowned."

† Senior Partner of the New-Brunswick House of Rankin, Gilmour, & Co.

Murdoch, being a Barrister at Montreal, and the other, Alexander, having held an appointment at New Orleans. A daughter, Mrs. Patten, lives in the Isle of Man.

2. Captain Kenneth McIver, of the Mercantile Marine, who commanded his own ship, and was the father of Murdo McIver, Esq. recently of Calcutta, and of Dr. Donald McIver, R.N.

3. The family to which belongs Mr. William Graham M'Ivor, the able and eminent Superintendent of the Government Plantations in the Madras Presidency. The grandfather of this gentleman, John M'Iver, who was of Lewis origin, and said to be connected with both the Gress and the Ness families, spent most of his life at sea, and died at Greenock, leaving one son and one daughter very young. The son, also named John, established the Nursery-Gardens at Crieff early in this century. He afterwards settled at Dollar, where he died, 6 Jan. 1860, aged 78, leaving :

    1. John, now at Greenhead, Muckhart, who is married, and has a son, John, and four drs. Janet, Mary, Christina, and Jane.
    2. William, Superintendent of Government Plantations in India,* b. 1824, married May 31, 1850, at Ootacamund, Anne, eldest dr of the late Colonel Edwards, Iseoed, Denbighshire.
    3. James, who died in India in 1868, leaving a son and a dr.
    1. Jane.
    2. Christina, who d. s. p. in India in 1857.

V. McIVERS in *British America.*†

Besides the members of the Coll family and others in Canada, there are many M'Ivers of Lewis descent in Nova Scotia, especially on what is called the Gulf Shore, between Pictou and the Gut of Canso ; also in the settlement of St. Anne's, and along the shores of the Bras-d'or Lake, on Cape Breton Island, where they are very numerous.

VI. McIVERS in *United States.*

Two highly respectable families from Lewis, of the Ness or Tolsta stock, migrated before 1812 to Chatham County, North Carolina, and thence removed to Madison County, Tennessee, from which some of them proceeded to the neighbouring State of Mississippi. One of the original emigrants had two sons, Roderick and John—the former, about 30 years ago, a prosperous planter near the town of Jackson, and the latter a member of the State Legislature. Mr. Roderick M'Iver removed to a plantation on White River, Arkansas. He was a severe sufferer in the late Civil War, in

* For extracts illustrative of Mr. W. G. M'Ivor's services, see Note at the end of this volume.

† For information regarding the MacIvers in America, the writer has to acknowledge his obligations to Daniel M'Iver, Esq., Stornoway, elder son of the late Dr. Alex. M'Iver, by whom it was acquired during visits to the United States several years ago.

which one of his younger sons, a Captain in the Confederate Service, and a grandson, were killed. His elder son, George, settled in Texas.

The Rev. Colin M'Iver, a descendant of the Gress family, was Pastor of Presbyterian Church at Raleigh, in North Carolina, and once held the appointment of Chaplain to Congress.

There is said to have been a Captain M'Iver in the U.S. Navy, and there are some others of the race in Georgia and Louisiana.

VII. McIVERS of the *Ross* Branch who continued on the Mainland.

Of these there were several families, as has been stated at page 44, some of whom can be traced from time to time, occupying respectable positions, and there are still some there and elsewhere in various places in the old Province of Moray, but no genealogical arrangement of any value can be made.

𝕰. GLENELG BRANCH.

Of this branch, which occupied a good position, but appears never to have been numerous, no genealogical traces having been found. Catharine, daughter of " MacIver of Glenelg," married, early in last century, Dr. Archibald M'Calman of Muckairn, progenitor of the M'Calmans of Drissaig.

The late Rev. Farquhar M'Iver of Glenshiel, although, it is believed, a native of Contin, was of a family which once possessed, as he informed the writer, the lands of Arnisdale in Glenelg.

𝕱. LOCHABER BRANCH.

The chief family of this branch seems to have been the M'Ivers, Campbells, or M'Glasrichs of Auchmaddie or Achavatie. On 16 May, 1749, " John M'Iver or M'Glasrich" is served " heir male general to his brother Angus More M'Glasrich or Campbell in Achavatie."

" John Campbell of Achmaddie in Lochaber," doubtless the same person, married Catharine, eldest daughter of John Macpherson of Strathmassie, by Jean, daughter of Lauchlan Mackintosh of Mackintosh, and had issue.

The author, named M'Glasrich, of some Gaelic poems, who lived in Perthshire late in the last or early in the present century, like all others who bear the same name, was probably descended from the Lochaber Branch of the Clan-Iver.

𝕲. PERTHSHIRE REMNANT.

Of these, no distinct genealogical information has been obtained later than the events referred to at page 18.

Extract from the " British Medical Journal" of 6th February, 1869, referred to at foot of page 82.

GEORGE MACIVER CAMPBELL, M.A., M.B.,

ASSISTANT-SURGEON H.M. 85TH REGIMENT.

" IT is with sincere regret that we record the death of Dr. George Campbell, one of the most promising assistant-surgeons of Her Majesty's service, cut off prematurely, in the midst of his duties, with every prospect of a bright and honourable career· The son of the respected Principal of the University of Aberdeen, living under the very shadow of the venerable pile of King's College, and passing several years of his life within its walls, Dr. Campbell will be remembered well by King's College men of a few years back. As a student in Arts, he conducted himself with no little credit, carrying off prizes in several branches of study, and graduating with classical honours in 1861. While studying medicine at the University of Aberdeen, he won the regard of all his teachers and fellow-students. He distinguished himself in nearly every branch, and concluded his curriculum by graduating with honours in 1864 as Bachelor of Medicine. In the following September, after the usual examinations, he was gazetted as staff assistant-surgeon, occupying a high place in the order of merit. After being attached for some months to the staff of the Royal Victoria Hospital, Netley, he served with the 67th Regiment, first in British Caffraria, and then, on its return home, in Ireland. In 1867, he exchanged into the 85th King's Light Infantry, and proceeded to India in the beginning of last year with that regiment.

" A serious outbreak of typhoid fever occurred in the regiment soon after its arrival, in which his services were found of the greatest value. He was shortly afterwards seized with remittent fever, and invalided to the hills, where he soon recovered, but on resuming duty there, he was attacked by " hill disease." Through characteristic devotion to his duties, the disease was greatly aggravated by exposure on a march in charge of a party of troops from the hill to Meean Meer, and assumed the form of dysentery, of which, after five weeks of severe suffering, borne with Christian faith and fortitude, he died on December 6th, at the early age of 26. Such is a short memorial of one who commanded the respect of all with whom he came in contact. Gifted with talents of no mean order, unassuming and unselfish in a marked degree, a thorough gentleman, and a man of sterling worth, Dr. Campbell will be long remembered with affection by his old fellow-students and regimental comrades."

Note relative to Mr. WILLIAM GRAHAM M'IVOR, F.R.G.S., referred to at page 108.

Mr. M'Ivor was born at Dollar, in Clackmannanshire, in 1824, his father having a few months previously removed thither from Perthshire. He was educated at the Dollar Academy, and began the study of Botany and Gardening in 1843. He went to Edinburgh in 1845, and thence to Kew, where he published works on the British Liverworts or Hepaticæ in 1847, and subsequently on the Mosses, and made some very interesting additions to the knowledge of the British Cryptogamic Plants.

Of his work on the Hepaticæ, Sir William J. Hooker writes thus in the " London Journal of Botany" of June, 1847 :

"A separate work was much needed on the Hepaticæ, and we have now the pleasure to announce an excellent little volume on these, the labour of Mr. W. Graham M'Ivor, at this time attached to the Royal Gardens, Kew. While resident in Scotland, and since his sojourn in England, this botanist has been indefatigable in his researches after these beautiful plants, and has consequently been eminently successful, and no less so in the accurate determination of the species."

In January, 1848, Mr. M'Ivor was selected by the Honourable E. I. Court of Directors to superintend the formation of the Botanical Garden at Ootacamund in the Neilgberry Hills in the Madras Presidency, and more than one Minute of the Governor in Council, as well as despatch from the Secretary of State, bears high testimony to the remarkable zeal, skill, and scientific knowledge displayed by Mr. M'Ivor in the important work committed to him, and to the success with which it was carried out.

In 1861, H.M. Government having resolved to introduce the Chincona Plant, by which Quinine is produced, and of which the supplies appeared likely to become exhausted in its native region of the world, into India, Mr. M'Ivor was entrusted with the whole charge of the plantations. In the fulfilment of this duty, he has, by devising new and improved modes of cultivation, effected results declared to be unparalleled in the introduction of a new product into any country, while he has contributed greatly to the knowledge previously possessed of the qualities of the different varieties of Chincona, and discovered methods of treatment by which the quantity of the bark and of the alkaloids which it contains will probably be largely increased.

These great services also have been publicly acknowledged in various ways by H.M. Secretary of State for India, and by the local Government.

The benefits to humanity generally, which must result from the propagation in India of the Chincona Plant, did not fail to attract the attention of other civilized nations as well as our own. Among the proofs of this it may be mentioned that an official complimentary letter from M. Drouyn de Lhuys, President of the Imperial Society of Acclimatation of Paris was received, and transmitted to Mr. M'Ivor, by H.M. Principal Secretary of State for India, accompanied by a large Gold Medal (Special) voted to him by the Society,

Mr. M'Ivor's talents have, as is well known, not been confined to the duties of his own particular department, but have been displayed in other great schemes and public undertakings, and the high reputation he has attained is felt to reflect honour on the race which is privileged to claim him as a member.

www.ingramcontent.com/pod-product-compliance
Lightning Source LLC
Chambersburg PA
CBHW022338020726
47500CB00004B/1182